T0284735

THE REVIEW *of* CONTEMPORARY FICTION

SPECIAL FICTION ISSUE: JUAN EMAR

SUMMER 2007 | VOL. XXVII

EDITOR

JOHN O'BRIEN

MANAGING EDITOR

MARTIN RIKER

ASSOCIATE EDITOR

IRVING MALIN

BOOK REVIEW EDITOR

MICHAEL SQUEO

PRODUCTION

SAMUEL J. COPELAND

REVIEW OF CONTEMPORARY FICTION
Summer 2007
Vol. XXVII

The *Review of Contemporary Fiction* is published three times each year
(January, June, September). Subscription prices are as follows:

Single volume (three issues):
Individuals: $17.00; foreign, add $3.50.
Institutions: $26.00; foreign, add $3.50.

ISSN: 0276-0045
ISBN: 978-1-56478-475-9

The drawings included in this issue are by Juan Emar, and appeared in the original publications of his works. Juan Emar's text and drawings published by permission of the Fundación Juan Emar.

This issue is partially supported by a grant from the Illinois Arts Council, a state agency, and by the University of Illinois, Urbana-Champaign.

Indexed in *American Humanities Index, International Bibliography of Periodical Literature, International Bibliography of Book Reviews, MLA Bibliography,* and *Book Review Index.* Abstracted in *Abstracts of English Studies.*

The *Review of Contemporary Fiction* is also available on 16mm microfilm, 35mm microfilm, and 105mm microfiche from University Microfilms International, 300 North Zeeb Road, Ann Arbor, MI 48106-1346.

Address all correspondence to:
Review of Contemporary Fiction
University of Illinois,
605 E. Springfield Avenue,
MC-475, Champaign, IL 61820

www.dalkeyarchive.com

THE REVIEW OF CONTEMPORARY FICTION

BACK ISSUES AVAILABLE

Back issues are still available for the following numbers of the *Review of Contemporary Fiction* ($8 each unless otherwise noted):

Douglas Woolf / Wallace Markfield
William Eastlake / Aidan Higgins
Camilo José Cela
Chandler Brossard
Samuel Beckett
Claude Ollier / Carlos Fuentes
Joseph McElroy
John Barth / David Markson
Donald Barthelme / Toby Olson
William H. Gass / Manuel Puig
Robert Walser
José Donoso / Jerome Charyn
William T. Vollmann / Susan Daitch /
   David Foster Wallace
Djuna Barnes
Angela Carter / Tadeusz Konwicki
Stanley Elkin / Alasdair Gray
Brigid Brophy / Robert Creeley /
   Osman Lins
Edmund White / Samuel R. Delany
Mario Vargas Llosa / Josef Škvorecký
Wilson Harris / Alan Burns
Raymond Queneau / Carole Maso
Richard Powers / Rikki Ducornet
Edward Sanders
Writers on Writing: The Best of The *Review of
   Contemporary Fiction*
Bradford Morrow
Jean Rhys / John Hawkes /
   Paul Bowles / Marguerite Young

Henry Green / James Kelman /
   Ariel Dorfman
Janice Galloway / Thomas Bernhard /
   Robert Steiner / Elizabeth Bowen
Gilbert Sorrentino / William Gaddis /
   Mary Caponegro / Margery Latimer
Italo Calvino / Ursule Molinaro /
   B. S. Johnson
Louis Zukofsky / Nicholas Mosley /
   Coleman Dowell
Casebook Study of Gilbert
   Sorrentino's *Imaginative Qualities of
   Actual Things*
Rick Moody / Ann Quin /
   Silas Flannery
Diane Williams / Aidan Higgins /
   Patricia Eakins
Douglas Glover / Blaise Cendrars /
   Severo Sarduy
Robert Creeley / Louis-Ferdinand Céline /
   Janet Frame
William H. Gass
Gert Jonke / Kazuo Ishiguro /
   Emily Holmes Coleman
William H. Gass / Robert Lowry /
   Ross Feld
Flann O'Brien / Guy Davenport /
   Aldous Huxley
Steven Millhauser
William Eastlake / Julieta Campos /
   Jane Bowles

NOVELIST AS CRITIC: Essays by Garrett, Barth, Sorrentino, Wallace, Ollier, Brooke-Rose, Creeley, Mathews, Kelly, Abbott, West, McCourt, McGonigle, and McCarthy

NEW FINNISH FICTION: Fiction by Eskelinen, Jäntti, Kontio, Krohn, Paltto, Sairanen, Selo, Siekkinen, Sund, and Valkeapää

NEW ITALIAN FICTION: Interviews and fiction by Malerba, Tabucchi, Zanotto, Ferrucci, Busi, Corti, Rasy, Cherchi, Balduino, Ceresa, Capriolo, Carrera, Valesio, and Gramigna

GROVE PRESS NUMBER: Contributions by Allen, Beckett, Corso, Ferlinghetti, Jordan, McClure, Rechy, Rosset, Selby, Sorrentino, and others

NEW DANISH FICTION: Fiction by Brøgger, Høeg, Andersen, Grøndahl, Holst, Jensen, Thorup, Michael, Sibast, Ryum, Lynggaard, Grønfeldt, Willumsen, and Holm

NEW LATVIAN FICTION: Fiction by Ikstena, Bankovskis, Berelis, Kolmanis, Neiburga, Ziedonis, and others

THE FUTURE OF FICTION: Essays by Birkerts, Caponegro, Franzen, Galloway, Maso, Morrow, Vollmann, White, and others ($15)

NEW JAPANESE FICTION: Interviews and fiction by Ohara, Shimada, Shono, Takahashi, Tsutsui, McCaffery, Gregory, Kotani, Tatsumi, Koshikawa, and others

NEW CUBAN FICTION: Fiction by Ponte, Mejides, Aguilar, Bahr, Curbelo, Plasencia, Serova, and others

DALKEY ARCHIVE ANNUAL 1: Fiction by Markfield, Szewc, Eastlake, Higgins, Jonke, and others

Individuals receive a 10% discount on orders of one issue and a
20% discount on orders of two or more issues. To place an order,
use the form on the last page of this issue.

CONTENTS

8   EDITOR'S NOTE

9   TRANSLATOR'S INTRODUCTION

FROM *DIEZ*

THREE ANIMALS

15   THE GREEN BIRD

29   THE OBEDIENT DOG

35   THE UNICORN

TWO WOMEN

57   PAPUSA

67   PIBESA

ONE PLACE

77   THE HACIENDA LA CANTERA

89   *ONE YEAR*

133   *contributors*

135   *book reviews*

THE REVIEW *of* CONTEMPORARY FICTION

EDITOR'S NOTE

Over the years, the *Review of Contemporary Fiction* has from time to time published "special" issues of original fiction or criticism. There are several reasons that such issues come about. It can be that an unexpected opportunity presents itself, or that a particular topic needs to be addressed—the "Future of Fiction" issue in 1996, for example. It can be that the *Review* is temporarily shifting focus in response to gaps we perceive in the literary culture, as is the case now with the series of anthology-style foreign-fiction issues we'll be publishing in the upcoming months (New Australian Fiction this fall, followed by Catalonian in the spring). Or, Dalkey Archive fills its publishing schedule, but then something comes along that we feel needs to be in print. Some combination of all of these stands behind this current issue of fiction by Chilean writer Juan Emar.

American readers can easily forget how little we know about the literature of other countries, not only about their contemporary writers, but about their literary histories as well. It seems strange, at this late date, to think that there are important figures in twentieth-century Latin American literature that remain virtually unknown in this country. In his Introduction to this issue, translator Daniel Borzutzky describes Juan Emar's own peculiar position in the history of Chilean literature, and provides some context for understanding how this surrealist/proto-"magical realist" has thus far slipped through the cracks. The bulk of the issue, the work itself, is intended as both an introduction to Emar's writing and, in a more general sense, as a reminder that the story of literary history—the story we tell ourselves about who was writing what, and when, and who else it might have mattered to—is always open to revision.

Martin Riker
Senior Editor
Dalkey Archive Press

TRANSLATOR'S INTRODUCTION

Juan Emar was the literary pen name of Álvaro Yáñez Bianchi (1893-1964). Yáñez, the son of a wealthy Chilean senator and newspaper owner, became Juan Emar while writing an art column for his father's periodical. He took the name because of its homophonic resemblance to the French phrase *"J'en ai marre"* (I'm fed up); and indeed, Emar had the right to be fed up: with the literati of Chile, who ignored his writing throughout his life and beyond.

Emar published three novels: *Miltin 1934, Ayer,* and *Un año,* all of which appeared in 1935; and in 1937 he published the short story collection, *Diez.* These works are now considered important milestones in Chilean literary history, but it wasn't until the 1980s and '90s that they began to receive the attention they deserved. *Umbral,* Emar's five thousand page magnum-opus, was published thirty-three years after his death, around the time presses began to re-issue his earlier books; translations of Emar appeared in French, Italian, and German; and critical essays and doctoral dissertations helped Emar gain what, in Pablo Neruda's words, in Chile "we are not stingy with— posthumous praise."[1]

To put Emar into context, it is helpful to examine the question of why he was originally ignored. Literary critic Nial Binns offers two explanations.[2] The first, writes Binns, was bad timing. Emar spent much of the 1920s in Paris, where he fell in with the *Grupo Montparnasse,* a collective of Chilean artists[3] inspired by the various movements of the European avant-garde, who polemically argued for an anti-academic, anti-realist, anti-naturalist aesthetic.[4] Emar returned to Chile in 1931, where he collaborated with, among others, the masterful poet Vicente Huidobro. By 1935, however, the Chilean avant-garde of the moment, due in part to events both national and international, was reaching its end. In 1932 there was a string of *coup d'etats* in Chile. Meanwhile,

---

1. See Neruda's introduction to *Diez* (Editorial Universitaria, Santiago, Chile, 1971).
2. See Binns, Niall. "En Torno a Juan Emar." *Anales de literature hispanoamerica.* No. 26, 2 (1997): 473-484.
3. Emar was the only writer; the other members of the group were visual artists.
4. For some basic information on this collective see "Grupo Montparnasse (1923-1930)" at *Memoria Chilena: Portal De La Cultura de Chile*: http://www.memoriachilena.cl/mchilena01/ temas/index.asp?id_ut=grupomontparnasse(1923-1930).

some of the stars of Chilean poetry, including Neruda and Huidobro, became involved in the Spanish Civil War. As Binns implies, the political climate led to a shift towards more "social themes" in the writing of the Chilean avant-garde. Emar's books, which are not in the least didactic, had the misfortune of appearing right as this avant-garde was dying.[5]

The other reason that Emar's books were ignored has to do with Emar's attacks on the most powerful Chilean literary critics of his time. He ridiculed them in his novel *Miltín 1934*, calling them superficial and boring.[6] They took revenge by ignoring him. Emar then retreated from the public eye, and spent the last portion of his life working on *Umbral*.

Emar, finally, was a figure of opposition, who personally attacked the literati of his time, and whose writing powerfully attacked the conventions of his time; and in "The Green Bird," Emar's most well-known short story, we see a narrator who embodies this oppositional stance both in who he is—a decadent young Chilean named Juan Emar who prefers "the Parisian nightlife to the more dignified Paris of La Sorbonne"—and by how he tells the story of an embalmed parrot who viciously comes back to life. The narrator's uncle curses the bird when he learns how it was acquired after a night of drunken revelry. At exactly two minutes and forty-eight seconds after ten on the night of February 9, 1928, the embalmed bird takes flight, mauls uncle José Pedro, and scoops out his eye. In the way the disembodied eye is described we see a microcosm of Emar's aesthetic approach, which melds joyous exaggeration with an impossible specificity, and which lands us in that awkward territory where horror becomes comedy precisely because of the obsessive way the horror is narrated:

> *My uncle's eye was a perfect sphere except at the point opposite*
> *the pupil, where a little tail stuck out, immediately reminding me*
> *of the agile tadpoles that live in swamps. From this tail grew a thin*
> *scarlet thread connecting up to the cavity formerly occupied by my*

---

5. Binns, 474.
6. Binns, 474

uncle's eye; and this thread, with each desperate movement my uncle
made, extended, shortened, quivered, but never ripped, and the
actual eye stayed motionless as if stuck to the floor. The eye was,
I repeat—with the exception of the deviations I have already mentioned
—perfectly spherical. It was white, like a little ball of ivory. I always
imagined that the back of the eye ball—and especially in the elderly—
would be lightly toasted. But no: white, white like a little ball of ivory.

Over this whiteness, with grace and subtlety, ran a streak of thin
pink veins which, when mixed with other cobalt colored veins,
formed a beautiful filigree, so beautiful that when it seemed to move
it slipped over the white moistness, propelling itself into the air like
a flying illuminated spider web.

By three minutes and fifty-six seconds after ten, José Pedro is dead.

Emar, undoubtedly, was ahead of his time. He is often classified as a precursor to the magical realists, for his writing anticipates the much imitated meta-fictional framing of Borges; and there are monsters, both animal, human, and other, roaming around his pages; and when seen as a whole his oeuvre is a labyrinth of interconnected characters[7] and worlds. And these worlds, as in the "June 1st" chapter of *One Year*, remind us that, from a certain angle, life is one big accident, and we are all utterly isolated in our ignorance of the ways we coincide.

The comparison to the boom writers, though perhaps inevitable, seems to me to be unhelpful and unimaginative. I'd like to think of Emar as closer in spirit to the great Chilean anti-poet and provocateur Nicanor Parra. Eschewing metaphor for the ghastly comedy of the surface while attacking the social and literary elite, both Parra and Emar are levelers and ironists who became major figures despite themselves. If Parra is Chile's anti-poet, then let Emar be Chile's anti-novelist.

---

7. These characters often have the names of Chilean towns (e.g. Longotoma, Atacama, Lonquimay, etc . . .).

Neruda, in his introduction to *Diez*, calls Emar "Our Kafka." And what I think he means, in part, is that Emar's writing, like Kafka's, defies interpretation by bringing us to a point where we think we understand, but where in the end all we understand is our lack of understanding of the many ways in which language and stories connect us to this world we hate and love.

Daniel Borzutzky, 2007

FROM *DIEZ*

JUAN EMAR

The Green Bird

This is what we should call this sad story. We will return to its origin, if there is anything in this life that has an origin.

This story began in 1847, when a group of French scholars arrived at the mouth of the Amazon on a schooner named *La Gosse*. They came to study the flora and fauna of the region so that on returning they could deliver a paper to the Institut des Hautes Sciences Tropicales de Montpellier.

At the end of 1847, *La Gosse* anchored in Manaos, and the thirty-six scholars—that was their number—in six canoes with six scholars each, went deep into the heart of the river.

Around the middle of 1848 they sailed to the village of Teffe, and by the beginning of 1849 they reached Jurua. Five months later they returned to this village hauling two more canoes filled with an assortment of peculiar zoological and botanical specimens. Immediately afterwards they sailed down the Maranon river, and by January 1st, 1850, they had set up camp in the village of Tabatinga on the shore of the aforementioned river.

Of these thirty-six scholars, I, personally, am only interested in one, which is not to say that I am ignoring the merits and wisdom of the thirty-five others. The one I am interested in is Monsieur Doctor Guy de la Crotale, 52 years old, chubby and short, with a bushy dark beard, good-natured eyes, and a rhythmic voice.

In regards to Doctor de la Crotale, I totally ignore his merits (which, to be certain, is not to deny them) and of his wisdom I haven't the faintest idea (which is also not to deny it). As to his participation in the famous essay presented in 1857 at the Institut de Montpellier, I am not aware of any bit of it; nor do I have any idea about the work the scholars did during those long years in the jungle. All of which does not nullify the fact that Doctor Guy de la Crotale holds a great interest for me. Here are the reasons why:

Monsieur Doctor Guy de la Crotale was an extremely sentimental man and his sentiments were situated, more than anywhere else, in the birds who inhabit the skies. Of these birds, Monsieur Doctor felt a deep preference for the parrot; thus once they settled in Tabatinga, he obtained permission from his colleagues to capture one, look after it, feed it, and even take it back to his country. One night, while all the parrots slept snuggled together, as is their custom, in the heights of the leafy sycamores, the doctor left his tent and walked between the trunks of birch trees, mahogany trees, and bead trees; he stepped on ferns, damiana, and peyote; entangled himself in the stems of periwinkle; smelled the foul odor of the mangachupay fruit; and heard the crackling wood of the buck-thorn. On a misty night, the doctor arrived at the bottom of the tallest sycamore tree; he quietly climbed it, stretched out a hand, and grabbed a parrot.

The bird was completely green except under its beak where it had two streaks of blue-black feathers. It was an average-sized parrot, about 18 centi-meters from head to the beginning of the tail, and from there about another 20 centimeters. Since this parrot is at the center of the story I am about to tell, I will give you some dates regarding its life and death.

It was born on May 5th, 1821, which is to say that at the precise moment its egg broke and it entered the world, far away, very far away, on the abandoned isle of Santa Elena, the greatest of all Emperors, Napoleon I, was dying.

De la Crotale took it to France and from 1857 to 1872 it lived in Montpel-lier, where it was painstakingly cared for by its owner. Later in this year the doctor died. The parrot then went on to become the property of one of his nieces, Mademoiselle Marguerite de la Crotale, who two years later married Captain Henri Silure-Portune de Rascasse. This marriage was barren for four years, but on the fifth it was blessed with the birth of Henri-Guy-Hegesippe-Desire-Gaston. From his youngest age this little boy exhibited artistic inclinations, perhaps an inheritance of his grandfather's fine tastes. This is why when he arrived in Paris at the age of 17—after his father was transferred to serve in the capital—Henri-Guy enrolled in the École des Beaux-Arts. After graduating with a degree in painting, he dedicated himself almost exclusively to portraits, and later, acutely under the influence of Chardin, he experimented with images of large still lifes with live animals. House cats appeared in his paintings amidst food and kitchen utensils; dogs appeared; chickens and canaries appeared; and on August 1st, 1906, Henri-Guy sat in front of a large canvas using as a model a mahogany table atop which sat two flowerpots with mixed bouquets, a little metal box, a violin, and our parrot. But the toxins from the paint and stiffness from posing quickly began to debilitate the health of the little bird, which is why on the 16th of that month it cast its last breath at the same instant that the worst of the earthquakes spanked the city of Valparaiso and sternly punished the city of Santiago de Chile where today, on July 12th, 1934, I write in the silence of my library.

The noble parrot of Tabatinga, who was caught by the wise professor Monsieur Doctor Guy de la Crotale and who died on the high altar of the arts in front of the painter Henri-Guy Silure-Portune de Rascasse, lived 85 years, 3 months and 11 days.

May he rest in peace.

But he didn't rest in peace. Henri-Guy sent him to be embalmed.

The parrot stayed embalmed and mounted on a fine ebony pedestal until the end of 1915, the date the painter is thought to have died heroically in the trenches. His mother, a widow of seven years, sailed to the New World; before embarking, she auctioned off most of his furniture and possessions, including the parrot of Tabatinga.

He was acquired by old father Serpentaire who owned a shop at 3 rue Chaptal that sold trinkets, antiques of little value, and embalmed animals.

The parrot stayed there until 1924. But that year things changed, and here are the reasons and circumstances:

In April I arrived in Paris and, with various compatriots, I dedicated myself, night after night, to the most extraordinary and joyful revelry. Our preferred neighborhood was lower Montmartre. We were the most faithful clientele of every cabaret on the rue Fontaine, the rue Pigalle, the boulevard Clichy, or the place Blanche; and our preferred spot was, without a doubt, *el Palermo*, where, in between the performance of two jazz bands, an Argentinean orchestra played tangos as sticky as caramel.

At the sound of their *bandoneones* we lost our heads; the champagne flowed into our mouths and when the first voice—a heartbreaking baritone—broke into song, we were on the verge of insanity.

Of all the tangos, one was my absolute favorite. It struck me the first time I heard it—it's better to say "I noted it," and yet, I think, I *isolated it*—a new emotional state passed through me, some new psychic element was born inside me, breaking and dwelling within me—like the parrot breaking out of its egg and dwelling amongst the gigantic sycamores—submerging itself, fortifying itself, and enduring the long notes of this tango. A coincidence, a simultaneity without any doubt. And although this new psychic element never shed light on my consciousness, it so happened that as soon as those chords broke I knew with all my being, from my hairs to my feet, that those chords were filled with deep meaning for me. So I danced, clutching my partner close to me, whomever she happened to be, with longing and tenderness and feeling a vague compassion for all that I myself was not, entangled with her and my tango.

And that baritone from el Palermo sang:

I have seen a green bird
Bathe itself in roses
And in a crystal vase
A carnation's leafless poses

"I have seen a green bird . . ." This was the phrase—in the beginning it was hummed, but later only spoken—which expressed all my emotions. I used it for everything, and for everything it was perfect. Later my friends started using it to describe anything blurry or ambiguous. For it encapsulated a whole range of secret codes and was flexible enough to fulfill an infinite amount of possibilities.

In this way, if any of them had big news to tell, a success, a conquest, a triumph, he would clasp his hands together and say joyfully:

—I have seen a green bird!

And if he were concerned or annoyed, in a low voice, with panicked eyes, pouting lips, he would say:

—I have seen a green bird!

It was used for everything. In reality there was no need to be understood; to express how much you wanted to entrench yourself in the subtlest creases of your soul, it wasn't necessary, I say, to use any other phrase. And life, expressed with this succinctness, took on a certain peculiar shape; it formed a parallel life which sometimes explained this life, sometimes complicated it, often filled it with an urgency whose depths we could not penetrate.

Later, after we got home from our parties, we would suddenly fall into uncontrollable fits of laughter at the mere thought of the words:

—I have seen a green bird.

And if, for example, I looked at my bed, my hat, or out the window at the roofs of Paris, that laughter, its tickle, poured a new drop of compassion over humanity, while scorning the unhappiness of those who have not been able, not even once, to reduce their existence to one single phrase which compresses, condenses, and even fructifies every single thing.

I should say, rather, *he has seen a green bird.*

And in truth, it could be that right now he is laughing at and understanding the desolation of humanity.

One October afternoon he went out to other neighborhoods. Visiting different bars in the afternoon and different *boites* in the evening, after a succulent meal he went home with a dizzy head, his liver and kidneys pumping energetically.

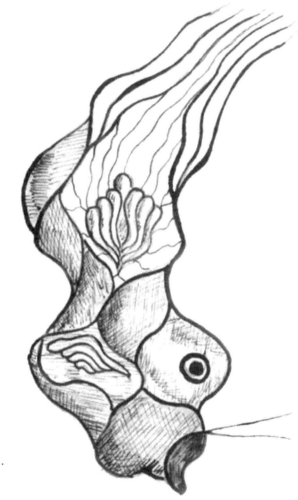

The next day, when at seven in the evening his friends phoned to meet for their nightly adventure, his nurse said that it would be impossible for him to accompany them.

They went around to their favorite places, and between champagne, dancing, and dinner, the sun rose and the magnificent autumn morning caught them by surprise.

With their arms around each other, singing the songs they had just heard, hats tucked over their eyes or ears, they walked down the rue Blanche and winded their way onto the rue Chaptal in search of the rue Notre Dame de Lorette, where two of them lived. And as they passed number 3 of the second street cited, Père Serpentaire was opening his little shop and appeared in the window confronted by the astonished looks on the faces of my friends, who saw before them, on its ebony pedestal, the bird of Tabatinga.

One cried:

—The green bird!

And the rest of them, more than amazed, fearing that they were in the throes of an alcoholic vision or a hallucination, repeated in a hypnotic voice:

—The green bird . . .

A moment later, after they recovered their senses, they rushed into the store and immediately asked for the little bird. Père Serpentaire wanted eleven francs for the bird and my good friends, thrilled to tears with their discovery, doubled the price and deposited into the hands of the stunned old man twenty-two francs.

They remembered their sick friend and went straight to his house. They ran up the stairs, much to the disturbance of the concierge, knocked on the door, and gave him the bird. And in one voice they sang:

I have seen a green bird
Bathe itself in roses
And in a crystal vase
A carnation's leafless poses.

The parrot of Tabatinga was placed on the work table, where he gazed out the window onto a portrait of Baudelaire on a mural outside, and there he accompanied me the remaining four years I stayed in Paris.

At the end of 1928 I returned to Chile. Safely packed in my suitcase, the green bird once again sailed across the Atlantic; he passed through Buenos Aires and the pampas, trekked through the mountains, arrived at Mapocho station; and on January 7th, 1929, his glass eyes, accustomed to the image of the poet, curiously contemplated the dusty porch of my house and, later, in my study, a bust of our national hero Arturo Prat.

The next year was spent in peace. The next in the same manner, bringing us to 1931, which entered with a terrifying bang.

And here begins a new story.

January 1st of this same year—which is to say (perhaps this date is super-fluous, but as I write it comes to my pen) 81 years after the arrival of Doctor Guy de la Crotale in Tabatinga—my uncle José Pedro arrived in Santiago from the saltpeter mines of Antafogasta, and when he saw that there was an empty room in my house he asked if he could stay in it.

My uncle José Pedro was a scholarly man, who believed that his most sacred duty in life was to give long didactic speeches to the youth, and he was especially fond of preaching to one youth in particular. His stay in my house provided precious opportunities. Every day during lunch, each evening after dinner, my uncle spoke in a soft voice about how horrible it was that I preferred the Parisian nightlife to the more dignified Paris of La Sorbonne.

On the night of February 9th, sipping coffee in my study, my uncle suddenly pointed his finger and asked about the green bird:

—And that parrot?

In simple terms I told him how it made its way into my hands after my best friends spent a night drinking and how I was not able to join them because the night before I drank and ate too much. My uncle José Pedro flashed me a stern look and then, perched over the bird, he exclaimed:

—Damned beast!

That was it.

This was the unraveling, the cataclysm, the catastrophe. This was the end of his destiny and the beginning of a total change in my life. This—I happened to notice the exact time on my wall clock—took place at two minutes and forty-eight seconds after ten on the fatal night of February 9th, 1931.

—Damned beast!

As the last echo of the "t" reverberated, the parrot spread its wings, fluttered them with a dizzying quickness, and took flight with the ebony pedestal still stuck to its feet; it crossed the room and, like a missile, landed on the skull of poor uncle José Pedro.

I remember perfectly how the pedestal, on landing, spun like a pendulum and struck with its base—it must have been pretty dirty—as it left a great stain on my uncle's elegant white tie. The parrot attacked his bald head. His forehead cracked, and out poured something like a stream of volcanic lava. It flowed out, bubbled, and a lumpy gray mass spilled out of his brain as trickles of blood ran down his face and left temple. Thus the silence that erupted when the bird took flight was interrupted by the most horrible scream. I was paralyzed, frozen, petrified. I did not know any man could scream in this way, let alone my kind uncle who always spoke so softly.

Intent on destroying the evil bird with one blow, I picked up the brass pestle from an old mortar and lunged towards the two of them.

Three lunges and I raised my weapon right as the bird was about to launch a second attack. But the beast restrained itself, turned its eyes towards me, and with a swift jolt of its head, promptly asked:

—Señor Juan Emar, would you be so kind as to do me a favor?

Naturally, I responded:

—At your service.

During my sudden paralysis, it launched his second attack. A new gash, new gray matter, new trickles of blood, and a new scream, but this time more stifled, more debilitated.

Once more my senses returned and with that came a clearer notion of my duty. I raised my weapon. But the parrot fixed its eyes on me again, and again it began to speak.

—Señor Juan Em . . .

Praying this would end quickly, I said:

—At your serv . . .

Third attack. My uncle lost an eye. The way one uses a spoon, the parrot used its beak to scoop out his eyeball, which it spat at my feet.

My uncle's eye was a perfect sphere except at the point opposite the pupil, where a little tail stuck out, immediately reminding me of the agile tadpoles that live in swamps. From this tail grew a thin scarlet thread connecting up to the cavity formerly occupied by my uncle's eye; and this thread, with each desperate movement my uncle made, extended, shortened, quivered, but never ripped, and the actual eye stayed motionless as if stuck to the floor. The eye was, I repeat—with the exception of the deviations I have already mentioned—perfectly spherical. It was white, like a little ball of ivory. I always imagined that the back of the eyeball—and especially in the elderly—would be lightly toasted. But no: white, white like a little ball of ivory.

Over this whiteness, with grace and subtlety, ran a streak of thin pink veins which, when mixed with other cobalt colored veins, formed a beautiful filigree, so beautiful that when it seemed to move it slipped over the white moistness, propelling itself into the air like a flying illuminated spider web.

But no. Nothing moved. It was an illusion born out of the desire—a fairly legitimate one, to be sure—that so much beauty and grace could exist, could come to life, levitate and captivate the viewer with its multiple forms.

A third scream sent me back to my duty. A scream? Not exactly. A weak moan; that is, a weak moan but sufficient enough, like I've said, to send me back to my duty.

A lunge, a whistle, and in my hand appeared the brass pestle. The parrot turned to look at me.

—El señor Ju . . . ?

And I quickly:

—At your serv . . .

A moment. Frozen. Fourth attack.

This one came down at the top of my uncle's nose and ended by its base. That is to say, the bird ripped the nose from his face.

My uncle was an extraordinary spectacle. Bubbling at the top of his skull, in two craters, was the lava of his mind; the scarlet thread quivered from the hollow of his eye; and in the triangle left by the absence of his nose, from the pulsation of his heavy breathing, a dense clot of blood appeared and disappeared, swelled and sucked.

Now there were neither screams nor moans. Somehow his other eye, from between its fallen eyelids, managed to shoot me an anguished glance. I felt it stab into my heart, filling it with all of the tenderness and all of the memories which I attached to my uncle. I turned frantic and blind. As my arms fell, my ears heard the sound of a whisper:

—El sen . . . ?

And I heard my lips respond:

—At your . . .

Fifth attack. It wrenched off his chin. It rolled down my uncle's chest and, as it rubbed against his elegant white tie, it cleaned off some of the dust left by the pedestal and in its place left a detached yellow tooth which shined like topaz. Up above the bubbling stopped, the dense gushing no longer appeared and disappeared around the nasal triangle, the thread from the eye ripped, and the chin, on falling to the floor, sounded like the beat of a drum. Then his two shriveled hands fell together and from his sharp finger nails, pointing inertly towards the ground, dripped ten tears of perspiration.

A soft whisper sounded. A death rattle. Silence.

My uncle José Pedro died.

The clock on the wall read three minutes and fifty-six seconds after ten. The whole scene lasted one minute and eight seconds.

Afterwards, the green bird froze for a moment, then extended its wings, fluttered them violently, and took flight. Like a hawk above its prey, it stayed suspended in the middle of the room, its trembling wings like raindrops on ice.

And with all of this the pedestal balanced itself to the rhythm of the clock on the wall.

Soon the beast circled the room and finally landed, or, better said, settled its ebony foot on the table and fixed its glass eyes on the bust of Arturo Prat.

It was four minutes and nineteen seconds after ten.

My uncle's funeral took place on the morning of February 11th.

As we carried the coffin to the carriage, we passed the window of my study. My family did not notice when I looked inside. There my parrot sat motionless with its back to me.

The enormous hatred emitted from my eyes should have weighed heavily on its feathers, even more so if we add to its weight the weight of the words whispered by my lips.

—I'll get you back, you filthy bird.

At that moment its head quickly spun around and it winked an eye and opened up its beak to speak. And since I knew perfectly well what question it was going to ask me, I winked back and, with a slight gesture, I gave it an affirmation which, if translated into words, would sound something like:

—At your service.

I returned to my house at lunch time. Sitting alone at the table, I missed my dear uncle's lectures on morality; I think of them every day and send loving thoughts to his grave.

Today, July 12, 1934, it has been three years, four months, and three days since my kind uncle passed away. For those who know me my life during this time has been the same as always, but in truth there has been a radical change.

Around my companions I have fallen into a complacency; whenever they want something from me, I bow and say:

—At your service.

And I myself have become so much more affable; before doing any kind of task, I imagine that task as a giant woman standing in front of me, to whom I bow and say:

—At your service.

And I see that this smiling woman slowly turns from me and walks away. There is nothing I am able to do.

But most everything else, as I have said, has stayed the same: I sleep well, I have a strong appetite, I walk happily through the streets, I talk enthusiastically to my friends, I go out drinking some nights and I have, or so I am told, a woman who loves me dearly.

As far as the green bird goes, it is here, frozen in silence. Every now and then, I offer it a token of friendship and in a soft voice I sing:

I have seen a green bird
Bathe itself in roses
And in a crystal vase
A carnation's leafless poses

It never moves and it never says a word.

The Obedient Dog

Desidiero Longotoma, Baldomero Lonquimay, and I are friends. This is not strange; we played together as children.

Did we really play games? Desiderio Longotoma and I certainly played games. What Baldomero Lonquimay and I played . . . I'm not so sure. Baldomero Lonquimay was, even as a child, extremely serious, and he was also . . .

I have written about his dark side elsewhere. To do so again would bore me.

When we were about twenty years old, Desiderio Longotoma bought a newborn puppy and trained it. He named it Piticuti. Piticuti was a small dog with a long body and a dark brown coat.

One day, Desidiero Longotoma told us:

Every pedestrian is an absurdity. When he is in his house or engaged in his duties or hobbies, every human being can be reasonable. But when he turns into a pedestrian he turns into an absurdity. We must fight against this absurdity!

So we did the following:

Each night, in a dark room on the lower floor of my house—whose windows were protected by colonial-style grates—we sat with the dog.

Silence. A long wait. My street was very quiet.

Soon a person came by. He passed the house. Desiderio Longotoma whispered:

—Zus!

Piticuti jumped against the grates and growled. The pedestrian coiled in fear. We did this every night for a month.

On another day he told us:

—All we are doing is attacking the heart of the pedestrian. All we are doing is instilling him with fear. No! We must punish the pedestrian with pain.

So the three of us took the dog out each night to walk the quiet streets of our city.

The sixteenth pedestrian we passed we marked as a victim; then the thirty-second, then the forty-eighth, etc. Always in multiples of sixteen.

On spotting a victim, Desiderio Longotoma whispered:

—Zus!

And Piticuti attacked his ankle. The four of us quickly escaped.

Each time we went out, Desiderio Longotoma would anxiously ask me:

—Who will be the sixteenth pedestrian? What will they be like? What preoccupations will they have had during the day? Which of those will have led them to walk the streets at night? If it is a man, will he have a wife? If he has a wife, does he love her? And if it is a woman? (for we did not absolve women; a woman who walks the sidewalks is as much a pedestrian as a man). On returning to her house, will she find a child ambivalent to her pain? Or will she come home to an old mother who will worry herself silly? Or two friends who will laugh mockingly? Or will her house be empty?

And Desiderio Longotoma would ask the same questions about the thirty-second, the forty-eighth, etc. . . .

Sometimes, as we walked the streets, we encountered different alternatives, which turned our anxiety to anguish.

We see the sixteenth pedestrian. He comes towards us, then turns around. It's not his destiny.

We see the sixteenth pedestrian. At the same time another pedestrian appears at a corner that is closer to us than the first, hence he becomes the sixteenth. He steals the fatal number.

It was his destiny; and not the first man's.

Etc . . .

Anguish suffocates. Anguish, like suffocation—if one studies it closely—gives pleasure. Which is what has been said by those on the verge of dying from suffocation. Which is why we are nostalgic for those times when we lived in the clutches of anguish. For those times brought us pleasure.

But let's resume, at least let's look at what's relevant:

In all this walking I felt suffocated by the presence of destiny.

Because I felt its reality, its liveliness to be like a monster which, though invisible, perched—fat, surly, silent—over the city.

It was a monster made of thread.

These threads knitted their way through the streets.

Each pedestrian left behind a thread which was sometimes like the silver excretions of the slug, sometimes like the fine web of a spider.

These threads could be seen the way one sees experience, the way one sees memories. I practically saw them with my eyes. I could see them in the space between my interior sight and my exterior sight.

I often saw them at the end of dark streets, quivering.

In the tip of each one, I saw a man, walking.

Each pedestrian cast another thread in front of him. This thread was barely visible, like a wish, like desire. Each thread, different from the previous threads, was threatened by the unexpected.

We were unexpected to all who walked the city!

We didn't make direct contact with any of them. We needed another creature of another species: Piticuti.

For me these threads were barely visible. In contrast, I felt them through my sense of touch, as if my body were pierced all over with long, fine spurs.

One night, I noted that they all pierced me, or spread down to pierce me on my sex.

I told this to my friends: Desiderio Longotoma laughed and laughed his quiet laughter; Baldomero Lonquimay was unshakable in his stone-cold seriousness.

I was able to communicate nothing.

And Piticuti continued biting.

After a while so much abuse started to weigh on our consciences.

To absolve ourselves we put together some money. The sum total we split in four equal parts to be divided amongst the sixteenth, thirty-second, forty-eighth, and sixty-fourth pedestrians.

We went to the poorest neighborhood in the city.

Piticuti stayed in the house.

I was amazed to find that I felt neither threads of awe nor threads of anticipation, nor threads through my sex.

I knew that giving charity was supposed to produce the same sensation as giving pain. I knew this . . . but nothing.

I do not know exactly what my friends were feeling. Baldomero Lonquimay said:

—It is not worth it to be so kind.

Desiderio Longotoma said:

—Enough of this nonsense! Let's get a drink.

And so the next night we returned to the streets with Piticuti.

On another occasion, Desiderio Longotoma told us with an air of mystery:

—I have a new project to carry out with our faithful companion. Tomorrow it officially begins.

But the next morning we found Piticuti dead.

We buried him in his owner's garden. Over his body we threw dirt. Over the dirt a cement gravestone.

Desiderio Longotoma fell into a great depression. He never told us his new idea. When we asked about it, he simply said:

—Why should I tell you?

And I never again felt the profound and passionate beauty of those quivering, nocturnal threads.

Poor Piticuti!

Twenty-three years later.

One week ago.

That feeling came back to me.

I was heading towards the hill in the center of this city. It was eight o'clock at night. I passed many pedestrians, cars, buses, and trams. Lampposts and neon signs flickered brightly. They made me feel dizzy.

On the left side of the hill is a labyrinth of twisting little streets complicated by the opening of new passageways and plazas and the construction of complex and enormous apartment buildings.

But I know this neighborhood well.

I was on my way to one of these streets with the intention of visiting a woman who both disturbs and attracts me.

Suddenly, a few meters from the hill, I went blind.

I stumbled for a hundredth of a second. All these little streets confused me, they so unexpectedly intertwined into an incredible entangling which stung me with the sensation that a mystery—dark, dreadful, effervescent—was bubbling throughout the neighborhood.

And the disturbing yet attractive presence of the woman I was going to visit was at the center of this mystery.

She lived it with the whole of her body. With her sex.

Despite my confusion, I continued towards her house and arrived like a sleepwalker, drunk on this beautiful anguish.

And as I walked I felt this whole neighborhood—with her at the center—vibrate in my sex.

The feeling came back to me!

For a hundredth of a second, nothing mattered.

That feeling came back to me!

And I realized that there exists a distinct relationship between the structure of a city and our most hidden desires. Which is like what I had learned years ago when the teeth of Piticuti taught me that there is also a distinct relationship between those desires and the strangers who walk the streets.

So I thought about returning to the tomb of our faithful companion and, as an offering to his memory, placing something on top of it.

But what?

I didn't know.

Everything I have ever thought to place there has seemed inappropriate.

Now I think that the best thing to do would be to place a snail on the gravestone. And to stand there, motionless, until the snail has crossed the gravestone from end to end, to stay there until the snail disappears from sight, far away, into the ocean.

The Unicorn

Desiderio Longotoma is the most absentminded man in this city. He felt obliged to place the following ad in all of the newspapers:

> Yesterday, between 4 and 5 in the afternoon, in the area enclosed by Los Perales Street to the north, el Tajamar to the south, del Rey to the east and Macetero Blanco to the west, I lost my best ideas and my most pure intentions, which is to say, my personality. A magnificent reward will be offered to anyone who finds it and brings it to my home at 101 Nevada Street.

That same day I walked around the indicated area. After a long search I found a cow's tooth in a garbage can. I did not hesitate a second. I picked it up and walked to 101 Nevada Street.

Eleven people were standing in line at Desiderio Longotoma's door. Each person held something in their hands and they were certain it was the human personality lost the day before.

The first one held: a little bottle filled with sand;

the second: a live lizard;

the third: an old umbrella with an ivory handle;

the fourth: two raw cow testicles;

the fifth: a flower;

the sixth: a fake beard;

the seventh: a microscope;

the eighth: the feather of a guinea hen;

the ninth: a bottle of perfume;

the tenth: a butterfly;

the eleventh: his own son.

Desiderio's Longotoma's servant ushered us in one by one.

Desiderio Longotoma was standing at the back of his living room. The same as always, cheerful, stout, with his thin black mustache, affable, relaxed.

He accepted all that was brought to him. In thanks he generously gave the following:

To the first he gave: a penknife;

to the second: two cigars;

to the third: a baby's rattle;

to the fourth: a rubber sponge;

to the fifth: an embalmed lynx;

to the sixth: a strip of blue velvet;

to the seventh: two fried eggs;

to the eighth: a small watch;

to the ninth: a rabbit trap;

to the tenth: a key chain;

to the eleventh: a pound of sugar;

to me: a gray tie.

Three days later I visited Desiderio Longotoma. I wanted to inquire into various matters which would be inappropriate to discuss here.

Desiderio Longotoma was in bed. He had placed over the headboard, in a wiry netting that stretched out to the middle of the bed, the twelve objects the twelve of us had taken to be his personality.

Beneath all of them, Desiderio Longotoma meditated.

(A passing observation: the cow's tooth was right on his sternum.)

This sheltered meditation reminded me of something that he himself had told me underneath a coral tree on October 1st of the preceding year.

After a long silence, Desiderio Longotoma had said:

—I would like to get married. I can only meditate in the shadow of something. I would like to get married so I can meditate in the shadow of two horns. I have been thinking about Matilde Atacama, the widow of Rudecindo Malleco, the failure. This woman, apart from being beautiful like no other, has become accustomed to intellectual love. Since I know nothing of intellectual love, Matilde would not hesitate to cheat on me. The only thing that worries me is who she will choose as her lover. For there are men who, on possessing another man's wife, cause the horns of the bull to sprout from the forehead of the husband; others the billy goat; others the stag; others the buffalo; others the elk . . . in short, all that zoology has to offer. And I want to meditate under the great horns of the stag. Nothing else.

I insinuated:

—Do you think that I . . . ?

He answered:

—Not a chance. You would sprout the single horn of the unicorn.

The unicorn lives in the jungles in the confines of Ethiopia.

The unicorn feeds only on the fragrant petals of sleeping water lilies.

Which doesn't keep its shit from stinking.

The unicorn, in its hours of relaxation, uses its single horn to dig deep caves in the soft earth of the marshlands. From the ceilings of these caves hang amber stalactites and hairy spiders on golden threads.

The unicorn will never be domesticated. When it perceives the presence of a human, it completely dissolves into thin air, except for its horn which falls off and stands straight out of the Earth. Then it buds prickled leaves and red fruit. This is what we call "The Tree of Tranquility."

Mixed with milk, its fruits become the most deadly poison if consumed by blossoming young girls. This, Marcel Proust was not aware of. Had he known, he might have saved himself several volumes.

The girls who die do not decompose. They turn to stone and stay this way forever. Any man who looks at them in their marble eternally loses all interest in girls who speak, breathe, and move through space.

I don't see any reason why the unicorn is contrary to the intentions of Desiderio Longotoma.

But he insists:

—The horns of the stag! Nothing else!

There was a knock on the door. In came an old lady. She carried in her arms a piece of clay stuck to the heel of a woman's shoe inside of which was one of Espronceda's verses.

Desiderio Longotoma thanked her warmly, and gave her in thanks a sheet of vellum and an oyster and, when the old lady walked off, he strung her offering to the tip of the ivory-handled umbrella. He repeated:

—The horns of the stag! Nothing else!

Desiderio Longotoma has married Matilde Atacama.

Matilde Atacama has taken a lover who has caused two enormous stag horns to sprout from the back of Desiderio Longotoma's neck. Now he can meditate in peace.

After his meditations, he did the following:

He bought a shredding machine, model XY6: eight cylinders, hydraulic pressure. He placed inside of it the thirteen things he was given when he lost his personality. And he shredded them.

He shredded them and crushed them until they turned into a fine, homogenous powder. He placed this powder in a hermetically sealed jar, which he exposed to five minutes of moonlight.

Meantime, Matilde Atacama was in the arms of her lover, and I was finishing my preparations for a trip to the confines of Ethiopia.

In Valparaiso I embarked on the *S. S. Orangutan*, and thirty-seven days later I disembarked in Alexandria.

From there I went to Cairo. A trip to the Pyramids.

At night, a trip to the astronomical observatory. I spent a long time contemplating the magnificent brilliance of Sirius and I remembered having seen it four years earlier at the San Cristobal observatory in Santiago. Then I gazed at the Moon. I also recognized its mountains, especially one that was like an enormous monolith, isolated, abandoned, in the middle of an immense desert which was like ice or milk.

Having realized this, I suddenly did not believe that Cairo and Santiago were two different entities in space. I was struck by the idea of spatial simultaneity. It was insinuated by Sirius and the lunar mountains; it intensified, consumed me while this white monolith passed before my eyes.

The next day, a second trip to the pyramids. Several times I beat on a stone at the base of the Cheops pyramid with the tip of my walking stick. In this way, with every strike, the idea put in my mind by the moon unraveled, and Cairo and the city of my birth became further separated by oceans and continents.

I continued by candle light on a boat down the Nile, then on camel through all types of highlands and, three months after leaving Santiago, I arrived in the confines of Ethiopia.

Two days of rhythmic exercises to acclimatize, and I was ready. And this is what I did:

I squatted at the foot of a birch tree with a jug of water on one side, and some regional bread on the other, on my head I placed an alarm clock programmed to go off as soon as I got tired, and at my feet I hung a wolf's tooth over a portrait of a nude woman which I placed on a sixteenth century chasuble. And I waited, waited, waited . . . 24 hours, 48 hours, 96 hours, 192 hours, and . . .

Slender, agile, graceful, whistling, luminous: a magnificent specimen of unicorn appeared in the greens of the jungle.

I needed to scream to get its attention; it would see me and vanish. I screamed:

—Look at me arrr . . . ! !

The unicorn came towards me, looked at me, and evaporated. And as its horn fell to the ground, the portrait of the nude woman began to frown and a macaw began to sing.

The horn fell, then stuck itself into the Earth. Minutes later it sprouted prickled leaves; hours later it sprouted beautiful incarnated fruits. I cut them off with a long pair of scissors, wrapped them in my chasuble; mission completed, I went to the Red Sea.

There a submarine was waiting for me. We returned through the depths of the ocean, passing beneath continents, which allowed me to make the following two observations. One: No continent, no part of the planet is grounded, everything is floating. Another: The Earth does not revolve around itself; the Earth itself is completely immobile in regards to its axis; what revolves is the cloak of water it is wrapped in and its floating continents; but the nucleus (that is, almost all of the Earth)—I repeat—does not move.

When I relayed this observation to the First Engineer, he looked at me awhile, smiled, then slapped me on the shoulders and walked to his cabin. A minute later he returned with a tennis ball which he spun between his two fingers. He asked:

—Does it or does it not revolve?

I responded:

—Of course it revolves.

—Okay then—he continued—it's the same with the Earth: in this ball, the rubber and the elastic band spin, so what does it matter what goes on in the empty space inside? The ball revolves and that is all that matters. To argue the contrary, my friend, is to get lost in subtleties.

—Allow me the following, Mister First Engineer. Let's imagine that inside of this ball is a smaller ball of wood. When you spin the ball between your fingers does the elastic exterior revolve around this inner wooden ball? Does the whole thing revolve? I say: No. And this is the case with the Earth.

—You are wrong, my friend. The Earth is like this ball and not like what you have imagined. There is nothing inside of it. Inside the Earth is a vacuum.

—Is that possible?

—Very possible. Give yourself the task of thinking a little: think that if there were something inside, that flame that is spoken of, or those demon and vermin-filled layers that your friend Desiderio Longotoma imagines, or anything else, do you really think we would be the sad and doomed beings that we are? Do you really think we would live the way we live, suffering our pains, miseries, and loves? Definitely not, my friend. A light would go on in our arrogant little minds. The inside of the Earth is empty.

I approached the First Mate. He said:

—You are correct. The inside of the Earth is completely immobile in regards to its axis, it does not revolve. What revolves is this layer of water with its floating solids.

—However—I ventured to insinuate—there are those who think that beyond these waters there is absolutely nothing.

—They are wrong—he responded. The entire interior is formed from a dark, compact, imperforable metal, a strong and silent metal. If this were not the case, if there existed only a giant hole capable of being crossed and traversed by birds and spirits, do you really think we men would be so pained and anguished? No sir. We would always wear a divine smile and the grimace of pain would be completely unknown to us. Inside of the Earth there is only a metal, dark and heavy, like destiny.

—Whatever the case may be—I said—there's something else I'd like to know, Mister First Mate: why is there a tennis ball on this submarine?

—That, my dear fellow—he responded—you will never know.

And with that he left.

Our trip continued. Twenty-eight days after taking off from the coast of the Red Sea, we passed below the Andes. From below we saw Quizapu, the enormous crater, which looked like a dark and decaying tube. As that moment took place at night, we saw above it, crowing it, a passing comet.

As we entered the Pacific Ocean, we rose for the first time to the surface. We saw a half mile south of us a boat, *El Caleuche,* with a crew of three dead witches. A discussion formed on the deck of the submarine. The First Engineer confidently declared:

—Those three cadavers are of the masculine sex, for as you all know, since *El Caleuche*'s inception, which is to say from the moment that God separated the sea from the land, it has been formally established that no dead female witches could sail on any of its boats.

The First Mate made a face and, while asking for the captain's binoculars, he solemnly said:

—One moment.

He looked for a long time. He then said:

—Mister First Engineer, you are mistaken. The third corpse, the one on the stern, is of the feminine sex. My friend (he said to me), see for yourself.

He handed me the binoculars.

In reality this cadaver was smaller than the other two, from its shameless cranium hung long locks which looked like the hair of a being who while on this Earth had been female, and beneath her rags one could see, in the soft substance of her breast, a jelly, and the ribs were not strong like in the other two.

These observations did not end the discussion. The First Engineer exclaimed:

—Mister First Mate, don't contradict me. My understanding of what goes on in *El Caleuche* is perfect. To prove it, see for yourself: at this exact moment it is 2:38. Okay, since there is a force-three wind from the northeast, and since there are only two clouds in the sky, and no fish in sight, *El Caleuche* should pass two hours and seventeen minutes after one of your ships staffed with three witches.

We waited.

At 4:55, we saw on the port side and beneath the water the glow of *El Caleuche*'s submarine lights.

The calculations made by the First Engineer were, without a doubt, profound. But the First Mate did not relent. He smiled maliciously. Then he called me to the side and whispered in my ear:

—The First Engineer knows a lot, an enormous amount, in respect to the relation of time and distance between *El Caleuche* and its boats, but of the sex of the cadavers aboard these boats, believe me, he is perfectly ignorant.

And with no further discussion, we went back inside the submarine and plunged into the water.

Two days later we arrived in Valparaiso.

I traveled by car to Santiago that same night.

At two in the morning I was in front of my house with the chasuble and the red fruit under my arm as the car hurried off.

And here begins another story.

Not even a minute passed before I was struck with an urge: to open the door with another key, enter on tip toes in absolute silence, to take long stops after each step, tremble at the sound of the mice and steal, steal as much as I could from my own house.

And that is what I did.

From a wardrobe I grabbed a big black sack in which to dump the stolen goods. I keep in my desk the skull of Sarah Bernhardt: I stole it from myself. In the hallway I have a painting by Luis Vargas Rosas: I stole it from myself. In the dining room I have two gold salt shakers: I stole them from myself. And in every corner of the house I have the complete works of don Diego Barros Arana: I stole them from myself.

I came to my bedroom.

At that time and on that day—had Desiderio Longotoma not spoken to me of the unicorn—I would have been in bed sleeping. At that time and on that day, if a thief had entered my bedroom after stealing half my house, I would have awoken, quickly jumped out from between the sheets, and shouted: "Who's there?" Thus I awoke and shouted.

If while robbing the house of an honest citizen I heard in the night his voice of alarm, I would crouch behind a dresser and wait anxiously, reaching my hand towards a weapon, in this case the sharp scissors that in the confines of Ethiopia I used to cut the fruit from the tree of tranquility. Thus I hid and armed myself. Silence.

Amid this silence, I screamed again: "Who's there?"

I gripped the scissors. My panting breath echoed off the boards of the dresser I hid behind.

From my bed, I heard his panting. Not a moment to lose! I jumped to the ground, took my revolver from my nightstand, and lights!

Seeing myself illuminated and surprised, I didn't hesitate. I jumped like a leopard with the tips of the scissors high in the air.

Seeing myself get attacked, I aimed and fired.

Seeing the mouth of the revolver, I made a quick move to escape. The bullet grazed my right temple and became encrusted in the mirror in front of me. Thus with all my might I struck with the scissors and stabbed my belly.

Wounded, scissored, I let go of the revolver and it fell as far as I am tall.

Which gave me the chance to stab myself a second time, and this time, I picked the heart.

Stabbed thus in the heart, I died.

It was 2:37 in the morning.

I backed away from my dead and bloody body with cautious steps. I remembered how Tosca backed away from the stiff corpse of Scarpia.

Walking backwards, I again crossed the threshold of the house. I inhaled once again the wet stench of asphalt. A name resonated in the silence of my mind: Camila.

I spent the night in a motel, repeating: Camila!

I slept.

The next day the newspaper announced my death in large letters, head-lining the article with the following words:

VISCIOUS CRIME

The following day the newspaper gave an account of my funeral.

Now that I was buried deep beneath the grass with the cockroaches and ants, the holy name of Camila, Camila, Camila resonated once again in my empty brain.

Thus I thought that the fruit from the tree of tranquility mixed with milk was what Marcel Proust had ignored.

Camila!

I dialed her phone number: 52061.

Camila!

What I always disliked about Camila, with her smiles and sarcasm, was her absolute ignorance. Camila, up until a few days ago, believed that the shells of almonds were created by special carpenters to protect the nut; that Hitler and Stalin were two figures intimately linked with our National Congress; that rats were spontaneously birthed from the furniture that accumulates in basements; that Mussolini was an Argentinean citizen; that the battle of Yungay had taken place in 1914 on the French-Belgian border. Camila lived outside all reality, outside all facts. Thus Camila was ignorant of the brutal crime and my sad burial. Which is why when she saw me arrive at her house she ran happily towards me and took me in her arms with the ease of a new little animal.

Then she laughed, and pointing to the chasuble under my arm, she yelled:

—Are you a monk?

Thus, before her astonished eyes, I unwound the chasuble and showed her the beautiful incarnated fruit.

—Do you eat it?—she asked.

After my affirmation, she took it in her hand and, with a long and wet caress, she licked it with her palpitating tongue. She then stuck her teeth in it. I stopped her.

—Not like that. You could hurt yourself. You must mix it with milk.

When you have been buried in a cemetery deep beneath the ants and cockroaches, all feelings of responsibility disappear.

These feelings appear and stab you when other men point their fingers at you in the street.

But if you are dead, there are no fingers that can enter your tombstone.

We both ate the red fruit. Except that she was a blossoming young girl.

I lay Camila's marble cadaver on the same table and slowly—finally—I took off her clothes. What she had just done moments before to the fruit, I did to her from head to toe. Later I stuck her in the black sack I had removed from my wardrobe. The sack was empty. For the stolen objects had fallen out onto the sidewalk as I walked from my house to the hotel, muttering the holy name of Camila.

I was out again on the sidewalk, beneath the wait of the marble. Back in her house, in the different rooms she occupied when she was alive, remained pieces of the sixteenth century chasuble and, on her bed, the sharp scissors.

Desiderio Longotoma exercises every morning. Afterwards he bathes in water which is 39 degrees. Then, for at least a half an hour, he rubs his chest and extremities with the fine homogenous powder produced by his shredding machine, model XY6, eight cylinders, hydraulic pressure.

—This is magnificent for your health—he told me as soon as he saw me. It is too bad you'll never be able to enjoy this because your memory is so strong. Because of my bad memory, I have no problems: no frigid winters, no scorching summers, no big meals, no strong drinks, no tobacco, no love.

After his rubdown, he dressed with great care. He put a flower in his buttonhole. He went into the living room. Lit a Cuban cigar. Kicked up his legs. Clapped his hands. He asked:

—What do you have in there?

The black sack fell.

—Camila!

White, cold, hard in her nakedness, and thus producing the maximum degree of pleasure.

After midnight, like two mysterious rascals, Desiderio Longotoma and I left 101 Nevada Street carrying—he from her feet, me from her head—Camila's remains. A third time on the sidewalk.

Halfway there, at my request, we switched positions. He took her head, I took her feet. For I have always found that Camila's feet offer much more to meditate on than her head.

An hour later we arrived at the cemetery.

Ten minutes later we found my tomb and through the stone we visualized the sordid rotting of my guts.

Desiderio Longotoma said a long prayer in a soft and hasty voice.

Then we stole the cross from my tomb and took it to the tomb of Julian Ocoa who had always been a good man and a distinguished violinist. We left it there since he never believed in God or Christ his only son.

Afterwards we went back for Camila, who had been momentarily left in the grass; we lifted her and stuck her little feet into the spot where only moments before the cross had been in the Earth.

This time both of us prayed with a cricket.

The next day the artists argued over the new sculpture.

Some found it to be a daring form of naturalism; some an exaggerated stylization. Some said it was of Athenian lineage; some, Byzantine; some, Florentine; some, Parisian. Some found it offensive to make the pubescent body of a virgin shine above those who were not virgins; some were certain that the nudity of a blooming young girl remedied the sins of those who slept under the Earth. Some left a thistle at her feet; some, an orchid; some a wad of spit; some, a bead of coral and mother-of-pearl.

I watched all of this from behind a Cypress tree. Desiderio Longotoma crouched in an empty grave.

Three days later no more artists came to offer their opinions about the sculpture Camila. Winter came and the rain poured icily on her pure form before the clouds.

Every day, two hours before the sun appears behind the Andes, I walk, with slow steps, to the cemetery.

I position myself in front of my tomb and Camila. I stand still, meditating.

I want to meditate deeply. I want to grasp death and all its secrets. But one floating image distracts me. An image I'd like to imitate, to reproduce so that my meditation can finally penetrate all of death's secrets.

It is the image of Hamlet next to the grave. No, it's the image hanging on the wall of my parent's house representing Hamlet next to the grave.

Because I imitate it, because all of this painting, my painting, is similar to the other one, on the wall, I do not penetrate any of death's secrets.

I only see Camila. I only ask myself who was right and who was wrong. Athenian or Byzantine, Florentine or Parisian. I only come to the conclusion that everyone was wrong because they all ignored what the statue standing in front of their eyes really represented. They are ignorant, and to substitute for their ignorance they want her to approximate a general truth: Athenian, Byzantine, Florentine, Parisian.

They ignored the fact that this was Camila, my beloved and wretched Camila; that this was her little body, always resistant to love and today to the gaze of others; that this was my complete transgression protected by a tombstone and turned to marble through my crime.

For a month I went to see her everyday.

The first twenty days I went by myself. From the twenty-first day on, I was accompanied by Desiderio Longotoma.

The fine homogenous powder from his shredding machine had deteriorated his inner pores and the good man was beginning to feel an attraction to the calm darkness of the cemetery.

—You are my audience, Desiderio Longotoma. No easy compliments! I want your honest opinion, your spontaneous opinion, Desiderio Longotoma.

—Okay, my friend, okay.

This, night after night:

I grab with my left hand a big clump of clay. Since the old lady visited Desiderio Longotoma, clumps of clay in hands have obsessed me. I attach to the clay an imaginary feminine shoe. Not one of Camila's, no. I stick in Pibesa's black patent leather shoes with the red heel. Because I have kissed Pibesa, especially when she wears these shoes. And since Camila never gave me her lips, now, in front of the image of Pibesa's high heels, I silently kiss she who is no longer of this world.

I point my fingers towards the statue and, as I touch it, I yell, spitefully, loudly:

—Here hung the lips that I have kissed I don't know how many times.

Where are your jokes now? And those flashes of happiness which caused roars of laughter at the table?

—Bravo! Bravo!—Desiderio Longotoma screamed frenetically—That is art!

And he laughs, for Desiderio Longotoma, above all else, shows his enthusiasm by laughing. You can hear his sweet, cascading laughter. Thus I become emboldened.

—What? Not a word to mock thy own face?

I make a large circular gesture with my right hand; as the clump of clay falls, and crumbles, the image of the shoe flies through the air. My tragedy reaches its maximum intensity. I say:

—*Alas, poor Yorick!*

Desiderio Longotoma, almost in ecstasy:

—Magnificent, my friend, magnificent!

And he laughs interminably.

This, night after night, for ten nights in a row.

And here begins a third story.

Cirilo Collico is a painter. He is a distinguished and talented painter. Without having or without ever having had even the least bit of audacity (you cannot expect from him even a milligram of novelty), it is impossible to deny that he has a certain sweet sensibility, almost feminine, as if it has been agreed—I don't know why—that he has what feminine sensibility is supposed to be. Cirilo Collico likes soft colors, light blues, violets, emeralds, light greens. He spends long hours contemplating the soft tones that time and rain drip onto cobblestones. A canvas larger than half a meter scares him. On sunny days he locks himself in his house. On cold days he walks the humble streets of the outskirts of the city emitting with each moment a tear of sorrow into the gray air. His ideal, his supreme ideal, is to paint the light of a diurnal lightning storm. Nocturnal lightning storms bristle his nerves and he hates them like he hates the sun, like he hates Rembrandt, like he hates Dante, and firearms, and the blood-filled lips of women with sustained gazes. In contrast, alone in his studio, beneath his skylight on a winter afternoon, Cirilo Collico trills like a note on a lute, suddenly his walls are illuminated with the soft, washed green of lost lightning.

Cirilo Collico is a detective. He is a sharp and shrewd detective with the eyes of a lynx and the speed of a hare. During these past few years there has been practically no scandal or crime that Cirilo Collico has not helped to solve. When the police are working on what appears to be a hopeless case, one of them always shows up at his studio to ask for help. Cirilo Collico listens, takes notes, studies, pokes around, goes out, runs around, interrogates, spies, deduces, surprises, and discovers.

It has been several days now since I talked about him with Javier de Licanten, the great bard.

—How do you explain—I asked him—such dualities in one man? Distinguished painter, delicate, sweet, nutty, at the same time a detective impassioned by blood and infamy.

—It's not that way—he responded—Cirilo Collico is, has been, and will always be a detective, nothing more than a detective, it is just a sinful inner shame—that nothing but blood and infamy interest him, that shame makes him pretend to be, in his winter studio, a parody of a man who is subtle and exquisite like almonds.

A little later I discussed Cirilo Collico with Doctor Linderos, the eminent psychiatrist. To my question he answered:

—You've got it wrong. Cirilo Collico is, has been, and will always be a gifted painter, and nothing more. And he is to such an extreme, to such an extreme he is gifted and to such an extreme he perfects himself more and more, that he himself has come to believe that if he continues like this he will become a being completely outside of reality, and this he greatly fears. So, to avoid this danger, he spends his moments of leisure submerged in a naked and cruel reality, which is to say, with blood and infamy.

—Whatever the case may be—I said—there is one thing I would like to know, doctor: why does Cirilo Collico insist on seeing me?

—That, my friend—he responded—you will soon know, that you will soon know.

And he walked away smiling.

Yesterday I ran into Cirilo Collico. We spent several hours walking the streets talking about painting, nothing other than painting. We didn't speak one word about his detective work.

On Zorro Azul street, amidst the bustle of pedestrians, we saw Desiderio Longotoma on the opposite sidewalk. On seeing me, he gave a secret signal and then, laughing, he shouted:

—*Alas, poor Yorick!*

I blushed. Cirilo Collico stopped me. In a serious voice he asked:

—What did that man say?

I responded hesitantly:

—He was talking nonsense, I don't know; I think he said: *Alas, poor Yorick.* That guy is crazy. Did you know?

Cirilo Collico:

—Yes.

A pause.

—Tonight you will be receiving news from me.

Another pause.

—Goodbye for now.

And he walked away with slow steps.

As soon as I finished eating, as I lit a cigarette, the doorbell rang. It was the postman. He handed me a small envelope.

I opened it and read:

> Cirilo Colico sends cordial greetings to his friend Juan Emar and he requests that he go, without delay, to his father's house, and that he examine the inside of his father's top hat.

I obeyed.

Minutes later I said to my father:

—Where is your top hat?

—Over there, on the wardrobe.

—Do you mind if I look inside it?

—In my house, my children can look wherever they want.

I walked towards it.

I looked.

There was nothing inside my father's top hat, absolutely nothing. What kind of joke or nonsense was Cirilo Collico's card? Then I felt my heart skip a beat and I realized I was turning pale. At the back, inscribed in the silk lining was the brand's logo; above, its name; below, its address in London; in the middle, the shield of Great Britain. That was what I was supposed to see.

The shield of Great Britain has a crowned lion on one side; on the other . . . a proud and magnificent unicorn!

That night I didn't sleep.

Today, at cocktail hour, Cirilo Collico came to see me. We sat by the fireplace. I called my butler. I was about to ask for a whiskey. However, I sensed that this called for something different, something from foreign soil, yes, from foreign soil.

—Viterbo, two ports.

We drank in silence.

Then Cirilo Collico said:

The Middle Ages were an extraordinary time period.

—Yes they were—I responded.

A new silence. A dog barked in the street. I yelled:

—Two more ports.

Cirilo Collico drank. Cirilo Collico told me:

—Read about the misfortunes of Dragoberto II, sovereign prince of Carpadonia in the years around 1261.

And he handed me an old leather-bound book opened to page forty. I read:

> And so it was that Dragoberto II, thirsty for blood, continued to pillage as the hooves of his wild colt trampled region upon region. As he crossed the peak of the Truvarandos mountains and entered into the green valley of Papidano, there suddenly appeared, above and to the right, the cross of Redentor, the oldest of the monks in the Holy Brotherhood of the Unicorns, and . . .

My voice got stuck in my throat. I coughed. I moved my feet.

—Damn!—said Cirilo Collico, looking at his watch—It's already time to eat. I am going, I am going.

From the threshold he said:

—Tomorrow we will continue the reading. Tomorrow first thing in the morning.

And he left.

As soon as I could no longer hear his footsteps, I snuck out of the house like a madman. I ran, and ran.

I arrived at the cemetery. I arrived in front of Camila. I prayed for the last time in my existence. This time a scorpion and a butterfly provided the chorus. Amen.

I opened the tombstone. And gently, I lay over my putrefied entrails.

Putrefactions have the tendency to ascend up to the heavens.

Mine ascend to the rhythm of centuries. They ascend uncontrollably. They ascend, filling themselves with interatomic interstices.

They have ascended out of the coffin. They have already gone out of the gravestone. They are touching the plants on the little feet of Camila.

They will always ascend.

They flood Camila.

Camila covers herself, from inside to outside, with my putrefactions.

Camila covers her holy body with a clear and odorous patina.

The artists from the city contemplate with rapture.

One says:

—It is the patina of Paris.

Another says:

—It is the patina of Florence.

Another:

—It is the patina of Byzantium.

Another:

—It is the patina of Athens.

Papusa

Belecebu's opal has been passed down to me through my ancestors. It was given to me many years ago; all of my predecessors were in their tombs and Belecebu had been dead for centuries.

When my father reached out of his coffin, I slid my left hand between the candles encircling him and, as soon as I felt the opal, I covered it with my right hand so that no particles from the flowers and cadaver would hide in its iridescent reflections. With a deep sadness, I lowered my head and left the fiery chapel, left the suppressed cries of those praying to God for the deceased. In my room I studied the gem, then put it in the drawer of my work desk where it has stayed ever since, idle as the ocean.

But last night, tired from my readings and meditations, I removed it from its glaucous ocean; I fixed my eyes on it and began to study its profound and mysterious inner life.

There inside sat the great and terrible Zar Palemon with his high court, his favorite servants, his jugglers and clappers, his gazelles and specters. There reigned, there thundered the fair and priestly Zar Palemon, reigning and thundering with his powerful voice of gold; he sat between the four pillars of alabaster; the faithful black Herculean Trabucodonosor split the air in a sparkling circle as he swung his tiger skin scimitar.

Silent, left to sort through thousands of dark premonitions, I studied the opal, and, slowly, before my eyes, a scene from this court unraveled, a solemn scene like a sacred rite.

Zar Palemon thundered, everyone turned pale, and the gold of his voice stung my ear drums. Trabucodonosor's scimitar cut through the air, a cool blast of wind hit my face, the red and black courtiers scattered against the aged gold of the great tapestries, the ladies shook their hot marbles and the clappers bowed, and beyond the gaze of my eyes the gazelles fled, so struck with terror. Only the specters remained still. They stood gracefully by their Lord and Master and fixed their hollow eyes on the ermine curtains trimmed with topaz and rubies.

A moment of waiting.

Then, from between the creases, a bishop appeared—this caused the jewels to tremble—an enormous bishop with an incommensurable miter, its pastoral staff radiant as a blaze.

Another moment of waiting. Trabucodonosor's scimitar sliced through the air, the jugglers and lackeys scampered, and the holy Zar Palemon, with his voice of gold, addressed the bishop:

—Let her go—he screamed.

A third moment of waiting.

The bishop pulled up his habit, which trailed down to the creaking floor, he stuck his hand into the fibers covering his belly and mocked and threw to the ground and displayed the sweet Papusa, her bronze hair, her inattentive gaze, her breasts, her sex, her imprecise smile which swung for several moments.

The magnanimous Zar Palemon shouted:

—Drop her!

Then the sapphire diadems on the sole of one of the bishop's boots struck and pierced the flesh of Papusa.

Papusa rises, steps forward.

She goes to the center. She stops.

The rug is purple. The air, sea-green. Nobody moves. Only the specters, who slightly tremble.

Fourth moment of silence, interminable. I wait with everyone else, with the merciful Zar Palemon, like his last servant.

And now I hear, I hear in a distant body of water, imprisoned in the sphere of the remote opal, I hear something indefinite, nearing.

It is the brave gazelles, approaching.

Galloping.

You can smell them from far away, and with all this terror there is still the naked skin of Papusa.

A sister, alone, thousands of eyes upon her.

The gazelles arrive. They stand tall and proud.

They look around. Their noses palpitate.

Zar Palemon puffs up his nose. Everyone takes deep breaths. The bishop, the specters, the clappers.

Papusa smiles shyly.

Then a long moment of waiting.

I wait with everyone else, with the magnates and puppets. Now I am engulfed and suffocated by those thousands of dark premonitions. I wait.

Papusa! My Papusa!

Zar Palemon rises. His armor expands and collapses like a gigantic wave. His index finger stabs the air. His voice rumbles:

—You, forward!

A courtier steps forward; he is young, blond, eyes sea-green like the air, dressed in indigo.

On the rug, Papusa spreads and opens her legs. She is on the rug beneath my lowered and heavy head; I stare into the gem on my work desk.

The holy bishop says a blessing while lifting his cloak.

All eyes are on the scene. Everyone is motionless, except Zar Palemon.

Zar Palemon is angry, restless, the pearls and flowers that hang from his throne crash into each other. He interrogates his specters with his eyes. They slowly shake their heads in disagreement.

Zar Palemon asks with his eyes:

—Should we attack?

The specters respond with their heads:

—No.

When the courtier stands upright, Zar Palemon thunders:

—You, forward!

He points his finger at a punchinello.

The punchinello steps forward, balancing his green and yellow hump.

Papusa falls.

The gazelles step backwards.

Papusa smiles shyly, her slight smile swings sweetly and innocently, enveloping the body of the punchinello, then rises, crossing the sphere, and spreading out, at last, across the walls of my room.

—Should we attack?

—No!

What attack is the all-powerful Zar Palemon planning? What do his specters see to advise against the attack?

I pick up a magnifying glass and place it over the opal. I watch carefully.

There I see the enormous, painted face of the court jester. There I see the sad, divine face, the sad smiling face of Papusa.

Nothing else.

We keep watching. We keep watching with all of our hearts and all of our blood. The scepters see something. We keep watching.

I begin to see.

There in the center, on the purple rug, under the yellow light, Papusa and the court jester are not alone. There is something else.

There is a swirl of gray smoke, spiraling and spinning out of the neck and temples of the punchinello, there is a small string of mother-of-pearls that starts to rise sweetly out of the bronze hair of Papusa.

It is what we both think it is.

We keep watching.

Entwined in the gray smoke is the most pleasure a man can attain. The pleasure of the entire body. The pleasure of revenge, of sanctity, when a man becomes deformed, monstrous, and lies down to make love to the beautiful young Papusa! I see flashes of dark red light come out of the gray smoke, they strike the impassioned spectators with hunger, the fury of possession. I see how all the people inside form one monster, one monster with a hundred thousand heads but only one thought, a hundred thousand hearts, but only one emotion, one hundred thousand sexes, but only one desire . . . Papusa!

Except for Zar Palemon, who is trembling. Except for the specters, who are silently going mad.

Except for the small string of mother-of-pearls.

Which comes out cleanly, without staining even one of its atoms. Shiny, strange, sublime. It comes out and at the same time is born in her bronze hair. Intoxicating, unique, pure.

Is Papusa completely frigid? Not even a quiver of pleasure . . . I understand, yes: *Not even a quiver of horror!*

Slowly I look away from this scene. I look towards the throne. Hiding behind one of the alabaster columns, I see the emptiness of a specter's eye sockets.

And so I ask, I ask with as much intensity as I can squeeze into one instantaneous glance.

And I hear the specter saying:

—Humans were originally sexless. Later their sexes fell onto their bodies, incrusted themselves, and those incrustations lived their own lives, nourishing themselves on the blood and ideas of humans. It has always been this way; and it will be this way forever. An almost eternal symbiosis that man refuses to recognize. A symbiosis he is no longer even aware of. Its abject identification is accepted without question. However, some who look sometimes question. And sometimes, it occurs to them that their sex lives separately, in cavities, slipping and crawling, on their bodies, men, women, royalty. Arrogantly, they say: "This is our will." They are wrong! They go crawling. And there are others—rare exceptions—who know what the truth is; they know it, they feel it, they live it. They have disconnected. There are two separate lives in one human, only in appearances they are one. But this, *this pact*, to be both human and sex, has been broken. Thus the sexes can live their own lives, nourished with a little blood, without ever making their power known. Remember a distant incident in your life, perhaps forgotten, but whose essence has remained with you, causing fear each time life has offered something analogous. Listen closely: can you deny that an "inexplicable" fear—in the space between cause and effect—strikes you each time you surprisingly discover life in an inanimate object?

"A dark night in the countryside; there is a rumbling of stones, distant like a phantom. Then, something from within the rumbling moves, appears, takes off. A dog. But at first thought it was, perhaps, a stone; in any case, life where you were not expecting it. And you turned pale, on the verge of letting out a scream. Life where I thought there was no life!

"Years before. A movie theatre. On screen an image of circulating blood. The globules, rushing, racing. Slowly something seeps into your understanding: the blood does not flow like a simple liquid, compact and impelled; there is life in each particle, alive, free. The globules race forward, stop, collide, agglomerate, search for their route, they search deviously for it, they find it, keep moving. Each one alive and living its life. An independent life, adjusted to fit into a greater life. Adjusted, yes, but independent. In your own body. You had to leave the theatre.

"A fear submerged deep into your childhood and which now when recalled in a certain way is like a pounding echo.

"A beach from your childhood. The shell of a sea creature, already opened. And you, looking inside as if it were the furnace of the Earth. Inside, dark like wine, viscous blue, the tongue of its sex, bloodstained, completely removed, sliced into pieces by a cold steel knife. The smell of salt water and sea caverns; a hint of aromatic putrefaction. Then, something inside bubbles, it lives independently, it sticks out six wet and pointy feet, stretches out and quickly moves. A parasitic little shrimp. Who you were not aware of. A scream of fear: 'Mama!'

"This fear was, in turn, a more hollow and distant echo. A fear born not in a sudden moment like the others, but slowly incubated during the stupor of discovering the life of the sex. A fear in the presence of the mystery of that sensibility, of that movement, which cannot quite be referred to as I; which, fearfully and disturbingly, we call him. A fear which—something sleeping, latent—exists alongside of our lives, causing us to vaguely ponder a strange duality, at times accepted, at times denied. A fear impacted. A permanent fear. A fear which *must* be our coupled destiny.

"And thus—like the rest of mankind—you have fearfully experimented in the presence of this intrusion which governs, which can govern and subjugate as soon as it takes control of the true center of your life, of your ideas.

"You doubt what I tell you. You doubt just like your fellow men who believe when they have a premonition and deny when it has been affirmed. Doubt if you wish. But first stretch out your hand; move your fingers: look at them. Look at how you are. Then see how you are both *him and you*.

"Zar Palemon wants this pact to remain strong in his subjects. Zar Palemon wants them to remain in this confusing threshold in which they sense a confusing duality but never go beyond it. Zar Palemon knows that as long as men are bound to this pact, they are virtually slaves, slaves to themselves, thus easily enslaved to others, which is to say, to Him, the fair and magnanimous Zar Palemon. His hand of iron is submerged in the sex of his subject, this is why he governs, this is why he thunders, this is why they tremble when the scimitar of the faithful black Tabucodonosor slices the air. Because there is not one free man, not one free woman, not one free gazelle in his vast empire. All of which is understood by Zar Palemon.

"Until one morning Papusa fell before his throne.

"Papusa is disconnected. Her sex lives outside. Her ideas remain safe. Papusa is pure and free.

"Think of what she represents, what she can come to represent amidst this vast empire, a human with a hold on her ideas . . . the beginning of the liberation!

"Zar Palemon cannot accept this. Zar Palemon concentrates all of his wishes into a great plan to reintegrate the sex and the free spirit of Papusa. Once they are reintegrated, he will submerge his hand into her, control her, subdue her, enslave her . . . the eternal and sublime glory of his powerful empire.

"Torturer . . . This is why she is nude in front of the entire court. This is why the young man went after her. But that was not enough. This is why she was attacked by the monstrous court jester. But that still was not enough. See her dreamy smile. See how her thoughts remain untouched, how with each attack they become more and more lucid. See how our Zar Palemon roars with anger when confronted with his impotence to entangle the sex of Papusa with her mind, to corrupt her, and once corrupted to subjugate her. Useless! Papusa is already free and no human power, even Zar Palemon, can succeed in afflicting her with the curse that all of us have submitted to.

"You thought of an abominable frigidity. There is no such thing! You see. Drawn into the mother-of-pearls, long scarlet locks.

"This is pleasure. Because she experiences pleasure like all other humans, like you, like myself thousands of years ago when I was a man. But in experiencing this pleasure, she remains outside, high above all the spasms, feeling them, yes, knowing them, without being them. That is why you see not even a quiver of pleasure, and you will never see even a quiver of horror."

And the specter fell.

Now the court jester stood up and disappeared into the multitude. Zar Palemon is standing, brandishing his trembling scepter. Papusa smiles shyly.

Me, leaning over, bowing, almost incrusted into the magnifying glass, shaking even more than Zar Palemon, but with indignation, desperately anxious to help Papusa and save her.

Zar Palemon screams:

—You!

A lackey takes two steps forward. Zar Palemon commands:

—The dogs!

A silence of expectation.

In the distance, in the remote distance, I hear galloping. They come closer. They bark. Here they are!

Great white mastiffs spotted with black.

The same scene.

The entire court shudders.

My magnifying glass shakes so much that everything becomes foggy and I can no longer see.

My magnifying glass falls. I collapse and fall asleep.

All that remains on my desk is the opal, which has been passed down from Belcebu to me.

Today I mounted it in platinum and wore it through the streets and plazas on my ring finger.

Today, as soon as night fell, I once again watched intensely. I yelled:
—Papusa!
There she is, alone.
—Papusa! Come! Give up the world of green and evil waters! Come to me! Forget what the specters say, leave that cavern! Here there is love, peace! Come!
Papusa smiles with her shy little eyes.
—Do you remember our past, our innocent childhood, our love?
—Yes, I remember.
—Then, will you come to me?
—No, I am completely faithful and obedient. If you want me to go, then He needs to tell me, my Master, the holy Zar Palemon.

Several hours of silence.
"Then He needs to tell me . . ."
Why should I even try? What interest can my life and my diminished love hold for the ever-great and terrible Zar Palemon, who in addition to his slaves has his court jesters, and in addition to his court jesters has his dogs, and in addition to his dogs he has to watch over all of his world, which he causes to shake with the little bullets he fires into my Papusa when her body slinks down, down, down?
In the solitude of my dark and dusty room, what interest can I hold for these transparent phantoms, for the unattainable mind of she who keeps an entire empire lingering in checkmate?

—Papusa! Give me something to hope for, just once!

—If He wishes, I will: if not, I won't.

If not . . . no.

No.

Zar Palemon has robbed me of Papusa; I gain nothing by carrying his whole empire on my ring finger.

Pibesa

We did not plan to go to the mountains. It happened by chance. We were walking the street one evening, bored and silent. I was kicking a wrinkled ball of rose-colored paper. For some time I kept kicking it in front of me. Sometimes she kicked it. Her name is Pibesa because she is quite young. She has a lanky figure and she does not speak unless I speak. But I know she is always paying attention to me. Proof of this: when one of my kicks left the ball of paper in her path she would kick it and send it back to my path. As she did this, the fine gray silk of her dress shimmered and beneath her dress breathed the beige silk of her knees. In the end I lost interest in her silk. We focused instead on the ball of paper, which had accompanied us such a long way. I picked it up and we read it. It was an entrance ticket to visit the mountains. It read:

Valid on today's date only.

Finally, something new, something to fill the emptiness of our lives. Something different: something other than our eternal walk down these tiresome streets.

—Should we go, Pibesa?

Pibesa blinked her eyes and trembled. Pibesa always trembles when you propose going somewhere. *To go*. Pibesa has concentrated all of her desire into the verb *to go*. The location does not matter. It is all in the act of going.

—Let's go—she whispered.

I looked at her closely, very closely, from head to foot. Her body as a whole did not tremble. She trembled little by little, she trembled in pieces, trembling in each part, in each fragment, until all of her body parts trembled.

We went to the mountains. We walked through galleries of snow, slightly green from the darkness. Soon we arrived at a large esplanade. We stopped. Behind us, the night stopped. There we stood in this eve of green snow. Behind us hid the silent blue night of sea above the sleeping mountain peaks. In front of us, beneath us, an afternoon of infinite mountain savannas, infinite as desperation, infinite as suicide. Further in the distance, as far as we could see, past the dead savannas, stood another single mountain range, undulating, bending, blinking red and orange against stagnant clouds.

—It seems to me, Pibesa—that there is something artificial in all of this, Pibesa. Don't you think? The night does not move forward (just as we do not move forward). The afternoon follows (just as we follow). The sun does not go over that distant mountain range (just as we are here and do not move). But to what extent can this serve as an explanation? I sense something artificial in all this, my Pibesa!

She said:

—Let's go.

I do not know if she said it out of prudence or to conjugate the verb *to go* for me. She did a half turn and took off running. I followed frantically. I ran towards her. I grabbed her with my left arm, wrapping it around her waist; with my right hand I lifted her gray silk skirt. And since she looked straight into the night, which is to say that her back was to the flaming mountains, this fire reflected off her burning blood-red skin. I tried to possess her jewels, I tried to possess her mountain blood. But Pibesa escaped, laughing like a rattle snake—she who never laughs—she escaped like a small, young animal.

I have always run faster than Pibesa. I catch up with her no matter where we are, no matter what the circumstances. And so I kiss her. Pibesa is agile, she is squirrelly, she is wound up in herself, in how to untangle and extend her life. When we run, she cannot figure out what to do with so much youthful energy and so I catch up with her, I pick her up, squeeze her and kiss her.

After my attempt at possessing her heavenly body, Pibesa ran. She ran and laughed like a rattlesnake, and I, eyes filled with red and yellow, began to realize how difficult it was to run along the green snow. I could barely move. It took all my strength just to move my legs. The earth did not give in response to my efforts. And Pibesa was getting further away, bouncing with laughter into the silent mountain peaks.

I do not know if everyone can understand how painful it is when you are unable to kick back dirt toward the abyss behind you. I do not know. I suffered desperately. I left behind the small part of the world I had just traversed; ahead of me was the enormous gap Pibesa formed between us. And what mortified me the most, with a mortification which forced me to deny the power of God Almighty, was that with the retarded weight of my feet, the snow did not have to do anything, nothing, nothing. It was an amplifying retardation, a retardation without reason and without snow.

My poor Pibesa! With her youthful laughter, she should have perceived my pain at not being able to run as fast as her, to catch up with her, seize and penetrate her, to burn my sex in the flames of her skin, flames stolen from the most distant of all the mountain peaks.

Pibesa stopped.

I kept running and in no less than an instant I devoured the distance that separated us. I then understood that it was Pibesa's speed that held mine back and not my weakness or the universe. Thus I remained in peace with the concept of my existence in the whole of creation, I yielded in silence and with fervor before God Almighty, and to Pibesa I said: "Pibesa, I love you."

Pibesa slowly descended the winding staircase.

Again I was struck with fear. What if when I descend the staircase that error in speed repeats itself? Pibesa had foreseen it all. Pibesa, bifurcating herself, split into two. Two young girls, with the youthfulness of water, wrapped in fine silk. One of them spun down the stairs, not too fast, no, but with such consistency, such certainty, such absoluteness, that I never would have been able to catch up with her. The other Pibesa moved slowly. With each step, her life stopped for a second, she stretched out a little satin foot and lightly grazed it on the next step. This is how she descended. And as she descended she hummed a slightly sentimental tune.

I made a second attempt at this slow, second Pibesa. Again I grabbed her from behind, lifted up her gray silk skirt and saw her skin, which, now shaded by the first flight of stairs, was silky blue. Thus I possessed her. When I touched her, she turned her head and we kissed; meanwhile, the second Pibesa descended slowly, very slowly, now humming the song that the first one had left in suspense because of the pains and pleasures that began to inundate her. I possessed her with my eyes closed, but soon I opened them so I could see my beautiful Pibesa. As I looked at her, she perceived me with a stupor which changed, which transformed as I went about possessing an unknown woman with all of my limbs. But it was already too late, I no longer had the strength to hold myself back, and, even though she was unknown, I had to empty myself into that incognito of my life which Pibesa, with the removal of silk, had sown during my impotent persecution.

For an instant, the mountains and the sky were erased and there was an absolute silence. Then one of my sorrows awoke one of her sorrows, and, as they shook together, the mountains and the sky returned, Pibesa's song echoed from the staircase.

—Let's go down the stairs—said the other Pibesa.

Pibesa waited for us a hundred steps below; she saw us and smiled. There was no irony in her smile, no compassion, no resentment. It was a solitary smile, isolated in the world. The three of us continued down the staircase without speaking.

Soon we heard the rhythmic echoes of heavy footsteps approaching. I felt an instant of horrible fear. I saw in the sound of those footsteps a man coming towards us.

—What?—I asked myself instinctively.

The rose-colored paper passed through my memory, the entrance pass. But this memory became quickly lost in a feeling of vague unease. I clearly had the entrance pass, there it was. However, this did not manage to soothe me. But this man wanted more than just my entrance pass. There was something that was not right, there had been something which had not been right. This I could sense. Something bad. And what frightened me even more, making each moment a moment of anguish, was the vagueness of this sensation. I should have instantly understood the consequences of possessing her, especially since she was not my woman. But no. This possession was neither good nor bad. What interest could this man have in her? She did not mean anything to me. She did not even care that I had left her at the top of the staircase. Then why did he care?

It was the totality of the situation which was wrong, there was something out of place, an exhaled breath—faint, but real—of near decomposition; in any case, of near decrepitude. Above all, the existence of the mountains we had left behind and above us. They were not in the exact point in which everything can be forgiven and everything can be allowed to continue. What fault was this of mine? It was not logical. But no logic could have explained the simultaneity of existence—however alone I may be in the actual moment in which I live—between the mountains, the sky, the staircase, Pibesa, the other Pibesa, and me. No one wanted to assign blame and responsibility and absolve me eternally. They simply told me:

—If you really have nothing to do with this, how is it that you are so precisely involved?

And the truth was that the footsteps of this man climbing the staircase were getting nearer.

I saw the tip of his Mexican sombrero spin down to my feet and disappear. I barely had time to grab Pibesa and shield her behind me. We stood between two pillars. If it did not occur to him to look to the right, we would be free. If not, he would see us, and, on seeing us, he would be as surprised as he was furious. The other Pibesa stood still in front of us, in the middle of the staircase.

The man appeared. With the same movement I made to grab Pibesa only moments before, this man grabbed the other Pibesa and they both disappeared.

In a soft voice I said to Pibesa:

—Let's go!

We started to run down the staircase. The echo of our footsteps must have been audible in the furthest corners, for we soon heard a powerful voice:

—Hey, hey! Who's there? Stop!

And we sensed how this man began to crumble.

I have already said that I run faster than Pibesa. Now, with each complete turn she took down the staircase, I took at least two, so that by the time she reached the foot of the staircase, I had already raced across the long corridor and turned into the entrance and was hastily trying to open the door. First I hopped over a chain, then removed two bolts and I was about to grab the key when from this same corridor I heard a gunshot. I moved quickly. The reverberation of the gunshot had not yet faded, but I had already opened the door and returned to the calm brown streets of my city. So I called to Pibesa:

—Pibesa! Pibesa! Have courage! We're saved!

I waited, trembling. Nothing. No one. Silence.

But soon Pibesa appeared in the entranceway.

She walked with a magisterial slowness and on her face she wore a look of indifference. Her right hand balanced like the pendulum of a compass that guided her tranquil walk. Her left hand held onto her waist.

As she approached me, she held out this hand. It was dripping blood. I then saw that from her waist, from the exact spot where her hand had been, her body was stained with a red that ran upwards like a glass being filled, and flowed downwards, like a glass being emptied. In this way the red of her blood swallowed up the fine gray of her silk.

I waited a moment. Nothing. I thought that the blood had stopped flowing and that its mission was only to saturate Pibesa's dress, for her neck was not red, the beige of her stockings was spotless and the black of her shoes was still like two pieces of charcoal. Suddenly her two heels, nothing other than her two heels, filled with blood; they turned scarlet and as the color dripped to the ground, the dirt surrounding her two feet, in a tiny space, slowly turned red. Thus I understood that the blood came from her skin.

Filled with indignation, I started to scream, to incite those around us against the wretch who had waged war against Pibesa, wounding and bloodying her. We were now in the middle of the street. Men, women and children stood at the doorways. I screamed:

—That man over there tried to kill her! That man over there, over there!

I pointed towards the open door.

I could sense that my indignation was spreading to the crowd. They emitted a soft rumbling, which grew louder. Barely moving their feet, just dragging them along, they approached the darkness of the open door. But when they were two or three meters away from him, to my amazement, he planted himself in the threshold and stood firm in the empty black space.

I figured he would run up the stairs to escape his inevitable punishment . . . No. He stood right there, in the threshold. He now had on a little derby hat, but he still wore his riding boots. He did not look at anyone. Out of principle, carefully, he studied me.

"They're going to cut him into pieces"—I thought.

I screamed:

—Stop the wretch right there!

Everyone stared at him with enraged eyes, twitching hands, ready to jump at his throat.

But he only looked at me. The crowd did not go forward. They waited for some gesture from him to provoke them more directly. Pibesa's wound was not direct enough for them; it was only direct enough for me. For them Pibesa's wound was only an abstract wound, a notion of a wound which angered them, to be sure, but which stayed on the surface and did not thrust itself into their muscles. This is what I thought. The man stood still and watched me. I kept screaming, inciting, pointing my index finger at him. The crowd began to relax, their hands were no longer twitching. Thus, under the persistence of his gaze, they slowly turned their faces away from him and interrogated me with their eyes. I forcefully screamed:

—Murderer!

With the same slowness their heads spun back towards the trajectory of

my scream, and their gazes fell, once again, on him. But I saw that they were no longer filled with fury. It was replaced with an astonished interrogation. And since he did not move, did not wink, did not breathe, for a second time the thousand eyes deserted him and swung back to me.

These people must have started to entertain the sinister idea that if this man carried all the blame, then he would be doing something other than standing there so still and silent. Desperately I moved my arms, forming a third attack. But I felt that I had lost ground, that in some place, some remote place, some unknown place, this man was at least partially right and the crowd recognized this.

A vague sense of guilt made me turn pale. None of my shouts were heard. But my eyes looked at him with such anguish that everyone, once again, turned around to see what effect I would have on him.

Everyone, myself included, watched and waited. He made his first move: with a cold calmness he reached behind his back, grabbed his revolver and with even more calm he pointed it at me, aiming from bottom to top. Everyone followed the weapon and they turned to watch me fall. At that instant I felt the blood filter out of my skin. The blood was green like the dead part of the mountain we had just visited, like the skin of the other Pibesa as she darkened in the shade of the winding staircase. And my last hope, which I felt nesting at the top of my head, escaped, abandoned me, flew off like a sacred bird.

But just then a police officer arrived; he confidently swaggered with both thumbs in his belt. He stopped in the center of the scene. He looked at the man with the gun, raised his right hand with his palm open and yelled: "Stop, don't move!" Then he looked over at Pibesa and me, and, with his other hand, as though tossing out garbage, he signaled that he was leaving. The man obeyed, lowered his gun, put it away, spun on his heels and turned around. Pibesa and I also left the scene. We moved quickly through the streets. The crowd dispersed. And the police officer walked away.

—Pibesa—I then said—this was all because of us. This is why we are fleeing, why none of these people will ever see us again.

An hour later we were in front of my house. I left Pibesa, went inside and ran down to the basement. The basement of my house has a small window. I stood there and watched Pibesa's feet walk by.

They went by.

I saw her gray stockings, her satin feet and her two sharp heels, bathed in scarlet blood.

The Hacienda La Cantera

I

For information concerning the hacienda *La Cantera* contact real estate agent E. Buin; 10th floor, Bank of the Pacific, any time, any day. He is almost always there, except in the summer when he takes a fifteen day vacation.

But all this pertains to my other book, *Miltin 34*, if memory serves me correct.

I, for my part, cannot supply major details, except to say that:

The property measures 849 square blocks, 208 of which contain rich soil and are irrigated naturally, 33 of which are irrigated artificially, 191 of which are small hills suitable for farming, and 417 of which can be used as seasonal pastures. There are many residential houses, administrative offices, bodegas, 2 silos, 9 apartments, 9 furnaces of galvanized iron and 16 of black iron, a large milk processing plant, a vegetable garden, fruit trees, and poplar and eucalyptus plantations. Total cost: $350,000.

In addition to this, *La Cantera* has cows, horses, sheep, pigs, and domestic fowl. For more details, contact E. Buin.

La Cantera has all that I have mentioned.

I, on arriving at the property (April 1st, 1935, 6:20 P.M.), noticed something else: a sign of disturbance.

The disturbance was between the leaves of the trees and dominated all of the inhabitants of the house and farm.

I felt the immediate need to remedy this disturbance. It came from the onset of a psychic putrefaction. The best remedy was to repeat the most basic actions which define our lives.

Three of us were present when the sun began to fall: (the wise and scholarly) Desiderio Longotoma, (the distinguished violinist) Julián Ocoa, and me.

The three of us wore black frock coats buttoned to our necks, black top hats, and gloves. We stood side by side, our elbows touching.

And we took off, steadily forward, but slowly separating at angles of 30 degrees.

There was something 125 meters in front of each of us:

In front of Longotoma: a tower of bricks;

In front of Ocoa: a step ladder;

In front of me: a pear tree.

We marched military style to our destinations: Longotoma to the tower, Ocoa to the ladder, and I to the pear tree.

Stop! One whole minute. And we started to climb at the same time.

From atop we watched the sun disappear. When it disappeared, Longotoma took off his top hat, held it above his head, and shouted:

—1, 2, 3, 4, 5, 6, 7 — 7, 6, 5, 4, 3, 2, 1.

He put his hat back on, and jumped.

Then Ocoa made the same gesture, and said:

—Do, re, mi, fa, sol, la, si, do — Do, si, la, sol, fa, mi, re, do.

He put his hat back on, and jumped.

Then I, in the same style, said:

—A, B, C, D, E, F, G — G, F, E, D, C, B, A.

I put my hat back on, and jumped.

We walked backwards the 125 meters to where we had started, closing in at 30 degree angles until we stood elbow to elbow with our backs to the hidden sun.

The day turned darker. But a few dusty specks of sunlight remained: green on the leaves, ocher on the ground, red in the flowers. An old man stooped over and swept the specks up with his broom. He threw them into his wheelbarrow and walked off with what remained of the sun. As he turned past some huts, night fell.

A metallic night filled the sky.

A faith blazed in our minds now that a basic order had been restored now that our disturbance had disappeared.

II

Metallic night.

A grapevine runs along the adobe walls behind the houses.

I am wearing white pants, a dark blue vest, and no hat.

I stop beside the grapevine, certain that he is there, no more than twenty steps in front of me.

I take a half turn and walk the other way. He takes a half turn and walks the other way.

I stop. He stops. I take a half turn, he takes a half turn. I walk forward, he walks forward. We approach each other until there are twenty steps between us. I stop, he stops.

Desiderio Longotoma has gone to his room and is reading: Plutarch's *Parallel Lives*.

Julián Ocoa, beneath an evergreen tree, has picked up his violin and is playing: Debussy's *Petite Suite*.

I stare into the night and feel the following sensation: vertiginous fear.

I hear the notes of the violin. The voice of Longotoma reports:

"The family of Cato derived its first luster from his great-grandfather Cato . . ."

I know that if I close the distance between us even one centimeter more, the atmosphere of our two disconnected worlds would mix and we would both end up sad and spiritless.

Ocoa plays his violin.

Longotoma:

". . . But afterwards, having proved his faithfulness and utility to Bruno, he died with him in the battle of Phillipos . . ."

And if my half turn is not matched by his corresponding half turn, then he will follow me. And if I escape, he will pursue me. I will get tired, and he will catch me.

I take a half turn and walk the other way.

He takes a half turn and walks the other way.

Metallic night.

III

I will always remember the exact time on my watch at that moment: 10 o'clock sharp.

Never in my life has this knowledge served any purpose, and, at that precise moment, all that occurred to me on seeing the time was that throughout my country all the clocks read 10, and in the neighboring country all the clocks read 11. In contrast, nowhere did the clocks read 9, except, perhaps, in the deserted waters of the ocean, if a wayward ship happened to be passing through.

Which was not very likely.

IV

A moment later all the anthills in the area exploded. And the walls, which for centuries had kept the ants imprisoned, flew through the air like birds flying through glass.

I was struck with fear, which, as is common when such explosions occur, produced a new and terrifying disorder which brought about the destruction of the entire hacienda *La Cantera*.

I ran.

There was no danger whatsoever. Because there stood Desiderio Longotoma and the cynic of Valdepinos.

Julián Ocoa had died.

Several friars carried his body. Against his chest, the violin; against his legs, the bow.

The procession marched solemnly.

A cross in the front swung like the mast of a wayward ship in the middle of a deserted ocean at 9 in the evening.

All the rats of *La Cantera* ran in the opposite direction, parallel to the procession; the ants had lost their anthills.

There was no danger whatsoever.

V

I saw Desiderio Longotoma and the cynic of Valdepinos.

Julián Ocoa was dead.

R.I.P.

These two men were in a large shed. The light there was ocher, the color of sand in a circus ring. The table was ebony, the chairs were white, the little ball was blue, and these two men were ochre, an ochre like the fading light of an oil lamp. Therefore, when I pulled a strawberry out of my bag, it created a beautiful harmony of colors.

Desiderio Longotoma, apart from being wise and scholarly, is short, fat, and has a mustache. The cynic of Valdepinos, apart from being a cynic, is tall, thin, and closely shaved.

They were sitting at the table, facing each other. Their balance formed a perfect rhythm: when the one leaned forward and touched the table with his forehead, the other straightened up and fixed his eyes on the roof (ceiling). This balance, with an absolute, perfect rhythm. These two men, and the space they occupied, emitted a perfect harmony, a harmony capable of resisting all the explosions of the world.

As I observed them, the rhythm and harmony strengthened: with each movement, Valdepinos said:

—*Tinguiririca*;

and Longotoma said:

—*Melancólico un quinqué.*

Tan, tan

tan, tan . . .

Absolute rhythm. Perfect harmony.

—*Tinguiririca.*

—*Melancólico un quinqué.*

So much harmony and so much rhythm rattled my nerves; as my nerves rattled, the blue ball began to roll.

It rolled on the floor, coming closer and closer to my feet.

I quietly left.

Despite their effect on my nerves, it was reassuring to know that the two men stayed put, finding order in the ochre light when they could have fallen into disorder.

VI

As soon as I stepped through the threshold:

—The widow! I said to myself, for the pointy old woman threw herself at me like a projectile.

—*Ay hijito!*—she said—I was such a close friend of your parents . . .

And she sent me back to when I was seven years old.

—*Ay hijito!*—she repeated—gripping my shirt collar—you used to call me Aunt Chacha . . .

My god! I was only two years old.

—And if only you knew why I always remember that day, the year that . . .

Crazy old witch! Crazy old witch who has returned to take me back to my mother's womb.

—*Hijito*, when I was a little girl, as young as your niece, I played with your mother, who was also a little girl.

Gloomy old lady, daughter of Hell! Return to the world of the dead and cackle like the sinister crows . . .

—I remember everything, señora, absolutely everything, Aunt Chacha . . . Please, please, let me give you five pesos.

VII

I continued walking through the night, passing blackberry bushes and malodorous herbs, walking further and further from the shed and the widow until I ran into two veterans leaning against the last standing apple tree.

Since the war of '79, they always met at the apple tree to talk.

They spoke of a coming war with a neighboring country and they expressed confidence that we would triumph, as they had triumphed. I stood behind a cherry tree and listened.

They then spoke of new wars and new conquests, which, by my calculations, would not take place until I was a veteran of the apple tree. With a soldierly gesture, and with the volume of a bugle, one veteran indicated to the other that a young man was in the area:

—There is no doubt, compañero, that when the grandchildren of that youngster over there . . .

And when the grandchildren of that youngster . . .

But, but what about me? Is it because I am standing behind a cherry tree that my existence flashes like lightning?

VIII

I continued walking through blackberries and malodorous herbs.

When I stepped on a stone, I felt blood beneath the skin of my feet. I remained, all the same, at the mercy of whatever evil had been let loose on the hacienda. Worse than exposing the nerves, the brain, or the heart is to expose the blood to that roaming evil which does not care for the unity of nerves, brain, heart, and blood.

That is the first danger.

Second danger:

With the blood exposed, I could be captured, as well, by any person I came across. If anyone so much as rubbed up against me, blood would flow out of my skin in thin sheets.

Nothing disturbed me, except for a quiet airplane which, more than disturbing me, disturbed the crickets in the fields.

Naked, I walked to the main patio, naked not only to the eye but to all of creation.

By now nothing remained of the metallic night. Now, it was a carbonic night, a carbonic night in the midst of which a tube sprung forth from the patio. Its walls were made of air. Its walls kept out the carbonic night.

Drips filled the inside of the tube until it gave off a leaden light. Because of this light, I could see them inside, talking in small groups.

We talked calmly, without danger.

Until I looked over to one side of the yard.

There stood two beautiful young women in rose-colored silk skirts, two silent, smiling, beautiful women who were looking right at me. And these two beautiful women had faces made of beeswax.

For a moment we stared at each other. And my blood transparently moistened my entire body.

The two women smiled with their wax faces. Their silk skirts whistled sweetly.

Their gloved hands held parasols that framed their smiles and the black needles of their gaze.

There were no more than ten meters between us.

In front of me, ten meters.

Behind me, all the meters of my past life.

In front of me, I repeat, only ten meters.

I couldn't overcome the distance by walking towards the women. All men stop when they see that there are only ten meters in front of them.

The mayten trees swayed as a soft wind blew. The wind blew towards me the distance I refused to walk. The two parasols also trembled, the smiles on the wax faces grew larger; the gloved women, gracefully balancing their silk skirts, walked towards me in a silent minuet.

As the women approached, I cried to all the gods to grant me extra meters of life, to extend me out in other directions, to extend me out past the surrounding night. But my cries were not heard and my body became nothing more than threads of external blood, threads which circulated outside of my skin, outside of my volition, open to all of creation, open to the wind that sways the mayten trees, to the kiss of the beautiful women, to the touch of their firm lips to my open veins.

Beautiful, melodious women. Their four sharp eyes stared at my neck, at a spot beneath my ears, and they began to walk towards me. One on each side, the wax of their faces submerged into my scattering blood, and I felt, in that moment of acute sensation, their black, solid, painted lips on my neck, kissing me, kissing me, and I disappeared within them, and I was erased into an abyss, in suffocating anxiety, my neck completely buried in their lips, as they, intoxicated, let their two parasols slowly slip from their hands like two flowers under the weight of the blood of their silk petals.

Silence. Total stasis. Only the bells of their skirts chimed softly. I closed my eyes for a moment. When I reopened them, their two faces were next to mine, grazing against my blood and staring at me intensely. They stopped smiling. Serious, inscrutable, impenetrable, they were two motionless masks. I could no longer see my friends with whom I had been talking, I could no longer see the yard and the mayten trees, I could no longer see their rose-colored skirts, their parasols, and their little gloved hands, and I became nothing more than a pale vision to their wax faces. And as they grazed the blood on my face, they continued to come closer, closer, and closer, until, in absolute stasis, their faces disappeared, and, for one moment, my two eyes, dilated in fear, disappeared, and their four stony black eyes, hooked into mine, had also disappeared.

Beautiful women! It was my last moment.

I made a grotesque face and laughed.

My laugh crashed into their beautiful faces. And when they heard my laughter, their own laughter echoed slowly, as they sluggishly leaned backwards.

Thus once more I was able to see their adoring faces, and I could see the silk of their rose-colored skirts; and I could see their gnashing teeth; and I could see my friends talking, and I could see the yard, and the mayten trees, and I could see, atop the roofs, the last leaves of a dying avocado tree. And so as I saw everything, once more, I could now measure the magnitude of my danger, and as the two women continued to look at me, one of them, without my having suspected, had started to lower herself upon me; slowly, her parasol, like a wide-mouthed pitcher, began to cover me, and cut me off from all the possibilities of existence, and close me off so that I was isolated, with only my blood and with their two firm mouths, behind their little ears.

But they leaned back and laughed, and, as they separated themselves, and opened themselves up, I imagined that I was a fan that was opening; and in this way I could imagine the moment of my salvation.

I waved my arms, and escaped.

Beautiful women of soft wax and elegant silk.

IX

I escaped, soaking up my blood with both hands, and trying to keep my skin from making contact with the air, until, at the edge of this night, I finally reached *La Cantera*.

I uncovered my skin.

Below, far below, with the dull sound of a rushing stream, I could hear night and day intertwined in a holy succession of the infinite.

Down below, night and day slid—light, dark; gold, red—and, like serpents of the Sun and of the Moon, they carried on their mission with all of humanity inside, with all its misery, happiness, and its cadavers.

Return! Return!—this was my hope.

Behind the damned *La Cantera*, entangled in the emptiness of this shattered nomadic night, I jumped into the abyss.

So long and farewell to all of it.

Now, falling, I managed to find a balance. I felt the whistle of a night which passed beneath me; then the clamor of a day which followed its destiny; and another night, and another day: the film, infinitely unraveling.

I fell.

X

The hacienda *La Cantera*.

For all pertinent information, contact E. Buin: 10th floor, Bank of the Pacific, any time, any day. You will almost always find him.

ONE YEAR

JUAN EMAR

January 1st

Today I awoke in a hurry. I did everything in a dizzying hurry: I bathed, dressed, ate breakfast, everything in a hurry. And quickly, I finished reading *Don Quixote* and I began *The Divine Comedy.*

I attribute this urgency to the *Quixote*, and to the date.

Yesterday, the 31st of December, the last day of a year, should have been, to be fair, the day I finished the last page of a book. But I didn't. I read:

> *A doughty gentleman lies here;*
> *A stranger all his life to fear;*
> *Nor in his death could Death prevail,*
> *In that last hour, to make him quail.*
> *He for the world but little cared;*
> *And at his feats the world was scared;*
> *A crazy man his life has passed,*
> *But in his senses died at last.*

I continued reading until a plump man sat across from me at my table. We looked at each other. Silence.

I lowered my eyes to read the first word of the following verse. The man pounded the table with his right hand, which I was forced to lift.

This happened fourteen consecutive times.

I have a certain affinity or a certain superstition about the number fourteen. I stopped. I did not offer a fifteenth. I closed the book even though I felt a brutal anguish as I saw the hands of the clock ticking towards the next year.

Today I finished it:

. . . thanks to that of my true Don Quixote, are even now tottering, and doubtless doomed to fall for ever. Farewell.

The sense of hurry, now nested in me, kept pushing me. I picked up *The Divine Comedy*. As if under a spell of vertigo, I arrived at the following passage:

Entrai per lo cammino alto e silvestro.

Now the sense of hurry forced me to leave the house.

I took the book with me. It's a big, heavy, hard-back book with illustrations by Doré.

With my book and my shoes, I ran through the streets.

A plaza. On one side a sturdy grey-stone building dominated by a huge tower. At the bottom, a small door whose threshold gave way to a staircase of the same grey-stone.

An idea: climb this staircase to the top of the tower, and stare out at the city and the distant countryside.

I did this. That is, I began to do this. I began to climb. But at the twentieth stair, I stumbled (what a beautiful word!) and *The Divine Comedy* fell from under my arms and rolled.

It rolled down the stairs. It came to the door, crossed the threshold, and tumbled through the plaza. It came to a stop near the center of the plaza, landed open on its back, wide open: page 152, canto 23. On one page, the text; on the other, an illustration: between two steep and isolated cliffs, on smooth ground, a man of the earth, naked, on his back, arms spread, spread wide, feet together, crucified, there on the ground, on the smooth ground, between the isolated cliffs.

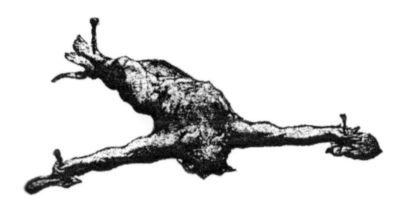

Dante and Virgil stared at this man. Beneath the illustration, the words:

Attraversato e nudo é per la via,
Come tu vedi, ed é mestier ch'e' senta
Qualunque passa com'ei pesa pria.

It began to rain. The water fell relentlessly. *The Divine Comedy* got wet, and oozed. The words melted onto the stones of the pavement. I climbed down the stairs, arrived at the book, bent over, reached out a hand and picked it up, hooking my index finger and thumb around the leather spine. I tossed it towards myself. Now, Attention!

Tenderly, slowly, I tossed it to myself. Arm, hand, and book began to shift with the slowness of a snail's nightmare.

My arm folded across my body. My hand moved back, and closed in. Its prey, the book, was also open. And with the book came the cliffs, the smooth ground, the two figures: Dante and Virgil.

Attention! Two figures. Not three. Because the crucified man, eternally crucified, did not come with them. In spite of the three nails, he slid around the page; more accurately, the page slid, the entire book slid out from beneath him.

A moment later, his feet slipped out of the base. His legs, his back, his crossed arms, his nape, hit the pavement with a loud thump.

The three nails sunk into his legs.

I walked back towards the door with *The Divine Comedy*, which was soaking wet, and missing one of its characters.

I looked: the good man was now growing, taking shape. A strong, muscular man, with a black beard and shaggy hair, naked, crucified, nailed to the ground in the middle of the plaza with rain pouring on him.

I returned to my house.

My sense of hurry disappeared. Now, as I write, I am calm. I am filled with an incomparable peace.

February 1st

Today I have had an extraordinary experience. Here's what happened:

But before I begin: my biggest joy is my magnificent tenor voice; and yet, I don't sing, and when I do sing I sing like a pig.

Ok, this was the experience:

I entered my living room, went to the mahogany cabinet, opened it, pulled out a file with some records, and then I took the needle from my phonograph.

I stood in the center of the room. There I pointed the index finger of my left hand straight—as straight as can be—up to the ceiling, while my other fingers stayed locked in my fist. Ok. Then with my right hand, I positioned a record on my left index finger in such a way that its hole fit exactly over my nail. Ok. With this same right hand I began to quickly spin the record, skimming its side until it spun with astonishing speed. Then I picked up the needle and with my right hand—arched and graceful like a swan's neck—I spun the first notes of the song.

And I opened my mouth.

I opened my mouth as wide as possible.

From my mouth, from my throat, from beneath my palate, over my tongue, echoing off my teeth and lips, deafening, thundering through the empty space, the voice of Caruso wildly sang:

> *Di quella pira!*
> *L'orrendo fuoco!!*

An incredible moment!

I repeated this experience. But with no results. I repeated this fourteen times. You already know what I think of the number fourteen. I didn't try, thus, a fifteenth time. Which is not to say that this was not a day worth living.

March 1st

Today I have been mourning. A great old friend has died. He died sitting on the ground, his arms crossed over his contracted legs, in a pose between mummy and drinker of maté.

When I arrived at his house, he was still alive. He sat in the aforementioned pose on the carpet of his living room. His entire family, his doctor, and various friends were with him, waiting. Everyone, naturally, was standing.

After a half hour of waiting, the doctor raised a hand, and whispered:

—Now . . .

My good friend then began to shiver. The doctor whispered:

—The last breath.

The wife of the unfortunate man then appeared. She stood tall, calm, and impressive.

She gracefully lowered her head. Many tears fell from her eyes. They fell on the back of my unforgettable friend's neck, trickled down and disappeared in his spinal column and into the pressed collar of his shirt.

The doctor whispered in my ear:

—Sit on all fours behind your friend. The moment he dies he will fall on his back. Collapsing on the carpet, plush as it is, must not be his first impression of death. Instead you must . . . Flesh upon flesh, my friend! Death with life! Jacket against jacket!

I was scared. It is not the same to see a man die in his bed as it is to receive him in your arms, to feel his jacket, beneath his jacket his sweater, beneath his sweater his shirt, beneath his shirt his skin that is no longer alive. Especially if you are perched on all fours, in the middle of a living room, surrounded by grieving relatives, still and silent like the sinister *alhuaquerecas*. It's not the same. And so I fled.

As I crossed the threshold, I heard an anguished cry and a muted thump: the cry of my friend's unfortunate wife, and the sound of the soft carpet receiving the noble back, the noble head of he who was always the purest of men.

April 1st

Today I took part in my irreplaceable friend's funeral.[1]

As I sat in my room weeping, the first stratum of my brain, the one next to the cranium, thought of how life without my friend would be a perpetual disappointment; meanwhile, the interior stratum thought of how these tears, once dried and solidified, would, if ingested with wine, undoubtedly produce a substance that would make me think that the death of my unforgettable and exemplary friend was of little importance.

That's what I was doing when I heard the somber chords of Chopin's funeral march. I said:

---

1. There is a strange reason why the funeral of my most cherished friend took place one month after his death, but this strangeness can be explained by the fact that his funeral did not take place one month, but rather two days after his last breath. Likewise, there is a strange reason why I have dated the funeral April 1st instead of March 3rd, but this strangeness can be explained by the fact that I have dated it this way because this is what the organization and construction of my diary requires.

—Here comes the funeral procession!

And I ran like a madman to join it. But I did not arrive at my destination. For the windows of my house, in the colonial fashion, have thick iron bars; I collided with one of them like a butterfly, like an insect with the radiator of a speeding car.

The door? Why did I not use the door?

My dear and old friends, you who are alive, if I knew why I ran to the window and not the door, you can be sure that at this moment I would not be writing, instead I would be relaxing, smoking in peace and not thinking about my dead friend, about you, or even about myself.

But I don't know why I ran to the window.

From between the bars, I looked down at the procession.

At that moment, the cavalrymen passed by. Grandiose, enormous, impressive: the cavalrymen and horses. They blanketed the buildings; they blanketed the sky. They marched in perfect formation, each with a wiry smile,[2] slicked back hair, an astrakhan hat over the right ear. Each rode a big black horse. But as they passed, they got smaller.

I could now see the sky. I could now see the buildings across the street. I could see them in their entirety. Now I was forced to look down, at the pavement, to see the strapping cavalrymen.

Until the last one passed; he was as big as a mouse.

The hearse then appeared; it was small, tiny, balancing like a ship in a tempest each time it crossed the groove between two cobblestones. And his relatives who walked on both sides of the car were like ants, like teeny, weeny ants.

My unforgettable friend!

---

2. Originally, I wrote "a stereotypical smile." Vicente Huidobro read it. He said:
—Don't write that. That is the sort of deadly expression used by those who want to be "literary." Write . . . write . . . wait . . . write "a wiry smile." That's what you should write.

I immediately changed "stereotypical" to "wiry." I did the right thing. "A stereotypical smile" is one of those phrases that has simply become commonplace (in the good sense of the term), as have—to use examples from this diary—"plump man;" "sinister alhuaquerecas;" "most cherished friend;" "colonial fashion;" etc. In practice, such a phrase can be used like any common words in the language. On the other hand, it is not a new image or as exact an image, as is, to my ear, Huidobro's sentence. And it is exactly in that bland middle ground that astonishes the latest pot-bellies and attracts the authentic literati.

I here express my gratitude for the good piece of advice.

May 1st

Today I crossed the threshold of my library. I had not been in it, not even once, for seventeen years.

It was full of dust. It was filled with a dim light that had darkened over time. An insect buzzed around the lamp, seventeen years! And on my work table, the *Songs of Maldaror* by the Comte de Lautremont.

I was overcome with emotion as I once again saw my bookshelf. It gave off a tepid warmth. Fading print clung to the cover of each book. Silence.

Silence, yes . . . And soon my ears, adapting to the silence, heard a trivial, trifling murmur; a murmur of piercing insignificance, an almost microscopic, yet implacable murmur.

I immediately understood what was happening.

Those vermin-bibliophiles, whose names I will ignore, those vermin who make their bread from abandoned libraries, were feeding on the words of the thousands of authors that silently formed on my bookshelf so that I— whenever the Spirit moved me—could release them from their silence and make them speak once again to my ears.

I opened the book by Lautremont and began to study it.

It had been attacked by only one vermin, no more than one. Its cadaver lay on the table, only a few inches away. Desolate cadaver in the plains, an unburied cadaver rotting in the dust. This is the story that had taken place when it was alive:

It began with the opening of an orifice in the back cover of the book, just in front of the space occupied by the last letter of the last word of the last line of the last song, which ends:

> It is nevertheless true that the crescent-moon shaped garments no
> longer take the expression of their definitive symmetry from the
> quaternary number: go and see for yourself, if you do not believe me.

The vermin had perforated the last e in "believe me."

Then he continued his slow and arduous labor, not as any superficial spirit would imagine it, and definitely not in a direct, vertical line. He continued in an oblique route up a slanting, inclined plane, treading softly, at a sharp angle, treading meticulously, precisely through this well-drawn tunnel of paper and ink, in pursuit of the first letter of the first word of the first line of the first song, which begins:

> May it please heaven that the reader, emboldened and having for the time being become as fierce as what he is reading, should, without being led astray, find his rugged and treacherous way across the desolate swamps of these sombre and poison-filled pages;

Here, the little beast perforated the first M.

And since the book was open, the little beast finally saw, after months, perhaps after years of grief and shadows, of the howls and curses of Maldoror, it saw once again the filtered light of my silent library.

It had worked its way through those 280 pages of "poisoned swamps" with a "wild and rugged" desolation and had received in its sleeping little body—like a new Christ for our modern day brothers—as much as a man can suffer trying to rebel and fight.

Noble little beast! Only once in its bleak pilgrimage did it see hope: in the second song, as it traveled through each page of the hymn to the louse. And when its simple nervous system received the voice that sang:

> And yet you still do not know why they do not devour the bones of your head, why they are satisfied with ceremoniously extracting the quintessence of your blood. Wait a moment and I will tell you: it is because they do not have the strength. You may be sure that if their jaws conformed to the measure of their infinite desires, your brain, the retina of your eyes, your spinal column and all your body would be consumed. Like a drop of water.

at that moment the little beast, from its dark prison, sent its "infinite prayers" of infinite honor up to Lautremont.

Everything else it experienced on its journey was exceedingly cruel. As soon as it completed its grueling work it started to run.

It fell from the book to the table. It kept running. But two inches later it imploded from pain and, on imploding, its microscopic soul was taken to the Great Almighty.

Noble little beast!

Today, I gave it a dignified burial beneath *The Song of Songs*.

June 1st

Today I experienced one fury after another, bouncing back and forth between furies, one fury, a second, a third, and so on.

First:

I left the house. A group of ragged old ladies were standing in line in front of the School of Advanced Polytechnic Studies. Certainly they were waiting for something, but what could eleven old ladies be waiting for at the School of Advanced Polytechnic Studies?

This question hit me like a projectile: What could they be waiting for? And that was sufficient: the fury dominated me.

I walked through the streets and passed the school: 1) enjoying all the privileges of freedom provided to each honest citizen of a model Republic; and 2) in full enjoyment of my freedom from the moment I awoke; I had decided to not formulate any questions in my mind.

However, after walking only one hundred meters, eleven old ladies nailed me to the sidewalk, keeping me from advancing and denying me my republican liberties; and then one question appeared before me, and called into question an assumption I had held for forty years: that I am a free man who only asks questions that he, and not others, wants to ask.

What could eleven ragged old ladies be waiting for at the School of Advanced Polytechnic Studies? First fury. It took a tremendous effort to move my feet from the concrete and continue my walk.

Second:

I moved my feet and walked. Alone. The pedestrians I passed slipped off me like ice. Alone, moreover, with my first fury. And a man alone with his fury is a danger . . . yes, a danger . . . but to himself, not to his fury.

I walked, then, to the house where my friends live.

The house has nine floors. On each floor there is an apartment. In each apartment lives one of my friends. In total: nine ascending friends: on the first floor lives a great friend; but on the second floor is an even greater friend; and on the third floor, even greater. Thus, as the floors rise, so does the level of friendship, until the ninth floor.

When there is absolute peace in my spirit, when not even a swelling can be perceived, I visit my friends on the first and second floors. And when some passion begins to stir in me, I climb the stairs in exact proportion to the potency of that passion. I rarely visit my dear friend on the ninth floor. But when I do visit him, our friendship extends, and explodes, like a powerful bomb.

After the eleven old ladies, I arrived at the threshold of the door of the house where my nine friends live. Calculations made and furies weighed, I decided to bypass the first, the second, the third, the fourth, and I rang the doorbell of apartment number five.

Cordial greetings. Then I explained to my great friend what had brought me to his house. He listened attentively. Finally, he said:

What a beautiful morning! Go out on the balcony. No discussion. Although you have walked quite a bit in search of peace, it is not the same, I assure you, as searching for peace while standing still.

I went out on the balcony. A beautiful morning, indeed. The beginning of winter. Cool air. And radiant sunshine.

Yes, sun, so much sun. Which is why below, on the streets and on the sidewalks, each man who passed dragged along his shadow.

Second fury:

Irremediably, a shadow for each man. Irremediably, a perfect imitation in the shadow of each movement of each man.

Fury. I will explain. I will explain the key to why this fury— of the shadows— attached itself to the other fury— the old ladies—without combining into one larger fury. There is an explanation for why the second fury remained atop and separate from the first fury, which was able to maintain its own force and presence, just as the second fury maintained its own presence. A double weight, a double anger. Now let us distinguish between them:

In the first case the old ladies were the pretext that inflamed my fury. But my complete fury relapsed, and the old ladies, somehow or another, remained outside of it.

My fury, perhaps, encircled me, without penetrating me, and I stayed within its sphere, free, calm, ignoring it the way one ignores the air one breathes.

The fury then collided with the eleven old ladies, and materialized in the form of an interrogation. It bounced off them. It became empowered within me because the interrogation enveloped me, squeezed the life out of me and asked me how it is possible that a sovereign man can be stopped by the first contradiction he finds on the street: the eleven ragged old ladies streaming out from the threshold of the wide door of the School of Advanced Polytechnic Studies.

The fury raged against me, a sovereign forty-year-old man.

But in the second case it is completely different. What fury could have affected me, isolated and unattached as I was on the balcony on this radiant morning? But I have an anger, a deadly hatred, of all the men who pass on the sidewalk, who walk from the shady side of the street to the sunny side of the street.

They walk past. They pass from shadow to light, from light to shadow. Like a spout of water that splashes feet, they spread a dark appendage against the luminous ground. They enter the shade: their feet suck up the appendage, which loses itself in the legs and disappears. This happens to every one, every single one.

I look at their faces. I have a small hope: that in at least a few of them, in two or three, there will be a small change in expression as they unravel in the sun, as their unraveling is sucked up by the shadow. Nothing!

They are preoccupied by everything, everything alters their physiognomy: another pedestrian, a car, a tram, a woman in her window, the newspaper, a cigarette, a dog in the street. Everything, except that which they spread against the ground, which they themselves absorb with their entire body.

Which is why this, amid so much else, remains inexorable: shadow in the sun, no shadow in the shadow.

They walk past. From all sides, in all directions. Their physiognomy changes at the site of a fly lost between cars and streetlights.

But nothing changes in the face of the inexorable. Not one gesture, not one little scowl. Cowardly men!

If, at the very least, one, only one man stood today in the center of the street, and protested at the top of his voice, his fists raised towards the sky, protested the unraveling of his shadow in the sun, protested the fact that his silhouette is not drawn resplendently in the shadowy pavement . . . But nothing!

Cowardly men!

I lash out at them with my mortal anger. Not at myself, a pure man, elevated in the frame of a friend's balcony.

Earlier against myself, now against the others. That is why the two furies are superimposed, each with its own force. A double anger!

And now, slowly, an old Victoria goes by at a short trot, with its old coachman, and in the front an old horse. And the three of them, coachman, coach, and horse, project upon the gold of the pavement three old and bluish dodderers who quiver with each slow trot . . .

The fifth friend on the fifth floor cannot calm my rage.

I say good-bye. I continue climbing the stairs. I ring the doorbell of my ninth friend on the ninth floor. Onward!

Third:

My friend doesn't say a word to me. With a quick gesture he directs me to his balcony. I go there: the beginning of winter, cool air and sunshine.

I do not look once more at the streets. I look forward, at another house, as large as the one I am in now. Windows and more windows. Through those windows I spy into the life of the other house.

Third.

That house across the street. As soon as I saw it, an idea consumed me, detonated within me: the idea of: "a whole." In this whole there were no parts, or if they existed, they were secondary. Floors, windows, walls, etc. . . . .

secondary. One house, one totality, one being. The house in front of me, fixed in a spot in the city, in the world. One house, an indivisible house. All of it following one destiny, to its proper and definitive end—which is, exactly, its destiny. Like my own destiny—the course of my life—which is a unified totality until my death. And if my right hand has a different destiny than my left, this difference is also part of one indivisible, unique destiny: mine.

In the house across from me, the same thing.

And for those who live in the house, the same. Because they belong to the house, the house includes them, and if any of them try to claim, all the same, their own existence, the totality always takes precedence: the house.

From across the street, I stand on my own. My destiny, my fate, is something else. I stand outside of that life current. I look on, alone and distant.

On one floor, merchants hard at work unfold and balance silks for a woman who touches and smells them. On a higher floor, several typists. Above them, exactly at my level, a family has breakfast: a man, a fat woman, a girl, and a little boy. And above them, and above me, every half minute, the bald head of an old man appears behind the glass and against the frame; sometimes I see his eyeglasses; less frequently, I see his white mustache, but always—every half minute—his bald head freezes for an instant, turns, and disappears into the ashes of his home.

A totality: the house, the destiny of the house with its globules.

Me: a different destiny, a different fate.

Thus:

Third fury:

I could see what they were doing. Yet they could not see amongst themselves.

The first was directed at me. The second was directed at others. Now this fury was directed at God.

And now I, on my ninth friend's balcony and across the street from the neighbors, performed, in miniature, like a louse, the role of looking into a world— though it was only a small part of a house— and seeing what those within that world saw only in sections. A small aspect of the role of God.

The old man of the half minutes! The moment, for example, when, approaching the window, he pressed his white mustache against the frame.

At that very same moment, the man on the floor beneath him coughed, and one of the typists on the lower floor swiftly flipped back her golden hair. So what?

Something, something large:

I thought of the last century of the human era. I then multiplied all the successive events that could occur, and I launched them beyond the earth, to the planets, to the entire cosmos, to measure them at the same time. An enormity of actions in an immensity of time.

But however enormous the actions, and however immense the time, the smallest, most miniscule actions are never, ever, in their fleeting, colorless moments, understood by those who take part in them. The actors never understand. But I do.

The old man never knew, never knew that at the moment his mustache appeared behind the window, a man, a man in his own totality, had released a cough into the air. And the man who coughed could not know—however much actions and times are exaggerated—that his cough occurred at the exact same moment when a woman flipped back her frothy golden hair.

This coincidence passed like a needle through these three points of action, forming a line which linked together these actions in one common and isolated instance, a line that will forever be ignored, even if we extend time and events beyond all possible calculations.

And I will understand this throughout the course of my own proper eternity.

At that moment the lady who touched and smelled the silks was standing still. If she had spoken, or lifted an orange silk, or if she had collapsed into an inanimate state, I would have known.

But the old man, never. Never would he know that his white mustache, which touched the wooden walls of the window frame, was in the same line of events, exactly the same, as the woman who had collapsed in the silks.

But yes, I would know.

The woman could have died. Her soul, carrying its virtues and sins, could have flown off to the throne of the Supreme Creator, to become undone, and to be seen and judged. Moreover, it could or could not have been that soul's destiny, to continue—its spirit traveling, suffering—ignorant that its undoing was in the same line of coincidence as the woman flipping her golden hair, as the man's jolting cough, as the mustache of the old man pointing towards the street like the teeth of a furious dog.

She is ignorant. I am not.

Something, yes, something large. It is something large to have had a bit —as small as it may have been—of God's vision of four people in one house in one instant who were "one" and who did not know of their union, and never would know.

It went against God. It made me feel—even though it was only for an instant, and even though it kept in check the minuscule nature of my existence—that I played a small part in His experience. But I want to continue in my role; I want to continue, without distractions or illusions, to be a human worm who slithers along, and who, when he senses his own helplessness, openly cries to the fires of Hell.

Not even my ninth friend could return peace to my spirit.

Nine floors in the opposite direction. Streets, long strides. A search for peace down another path.

July 1st

Today I wandered aimlessly. Behind me, at each step, the finger of God. I have felt it at every moment. Twice it stuck into my neck.

He did this lightly, as if mistakenly. Like a glimpse of a glimpse, entwining me in my own ideas about his identity.

This is what happened:

I was walking along a busy central boulevard. Suddenly, there was an accident: a carriage and a car collided. Commotion, vociferations, and so on. Two men slapped each other. Injuries, one death, Public Assistants, police officers. For a moment I thought this was going to change the direction of the entire city, and thus the entire nation. But in one minute, perhaps less, everything was calm. The disturbance disappeared like a magic trick: arguments, police officers, Public Assistants, curious bystanders, everything. The boulevard's normal circulation returned without absorbing even a trace of what had occurred.

And just as the street had returned to its normal appearance, Estanislao Brun, walking in long, loud strides, appeared at one corner, with his little gold glasses and his curved back and his briefcase of stocks and bonds tucked beneath his arm. And he walked past.

He walked past—what!—and then walked over, trampling, clicking his heels, on the very site, the exact spot where, only seconds earlier, the two vehicles had collided, the men had slapped each other, the injuries had occurred, where someone had died, and where the public order had dissolved. And he walked past, I repeat, that same spot, step by step, without noticing a thing, without smelling a thing, practically erasing the existence of the accident, an unlikely being coasting along, one millimeter from, a half millimeter from a sensational act, which he had no idea about, and which he never would know about.

For twenty minutes I stood still on the corner without understanding, or, more accurately, understanding as absurdity these paths of destiny, these winding threads that intertwine but never make contact, each one lost in its own world of ignorance, side by side, in a world of not-knowing.

I continued to wander around. Now I am walking down a quiet street, with little gardens on one side, small residential houses on the other. One of these houses: a friend's house, an acquaintance, really, whose name I will not reveal for the simple reason that I consider him to be perfectly unfriendly, and because I consider him to be one of the most illustrious examples of our imbecility.

It is 3:32 in the afternoon. The upstairs windows of his study are closed, the downstairs windows are open. An unmistakable sign that the man in question is inside. Moreover, there are other signs that he is there. There can be no doubt that he is inside.

Ok. This character wants to see me, needs to see me, my presence or absence could alter, for better or worse, his destiny. But various circumstances (about which I must keep quiet) oblige us to meet each other by mere chance, and nothing else. There is no room for any other option.

In summary: he is inside; I am on the street, walking.

I walk past his house, slowly.

I am his destiny, a possible change in his destiny that he desires and needs.

It is exactly 3:33. I am in front of his window. Behind it, the man is submerged in his old parchment papers. I walk past.

I pass, and move away from the house. Now I am outside of, and far from, his orbit.

He has no idea what slow, parallel thread of destiny just passed him, one step forward, would have entwined the various lines that have twisted through his existence.

He has no idea. None! Not even the slightest vibration on one page of his old parchment papers. Not even an inopportune insect that causes him, exactly at 3:33, to break from his work and make a different gesture. Nothing!

I pass his house, with the finger of God on my neck, pushing me forward. Twice the finger of God. The effect: exhaustion, fatigue.

But in the evening, this evening, a distraction will come, a rest. The cynic of Valdepinos will have dinner with my brother Pedro and myself. Cynical he may be, but his conversation, in all its cynicism, nonetheless diminishes my worries, and brings peace.

At exactly nine on the dot the tall figure of the cynic of Valdepinos came to the door.

Before I continue:

There are two things, two entities which should always be united, or which—to state it better—should have always remained united. Alas, destiny has thrown them from one side of the Earth to the other and does not allow them to be together, for one of them is in the beautiful country of Chile, while the other cannot find a way of leaving the sweet land of France: the cynic of Valdepinos is here; Pernod, is there.

But this is in principle, as if someone declared it "the Law." In reality, in a loose and dying reality, life does not always follow the rule of law: some time ago, a friend who lives in Paris sent me two bottles of Pernod.

The first one was finished months ago, but the second has been distilled slowly. To this day, I store half of its contents (I keep half of its contents hidden). A half which must be defended, like the land of honor, drop by drop! As if the bottle's final drop will be the last to ever spill in the history of Chile.

The cynic of Valdepinos eats and talks. Behind him, a cabinet which hides in one of its compartments the final half liter: thick, silent, like opal. If the cynic of Valdepinos knew!

We eat, we talk. But from time to time I sense something uncomfortable passing above our plates.

Pedro is struck by a memory: in the same cabinet, near the back, he once stored an aged bottle of red wine. He gets up in a storm, opens the cabinet, sticks his hand in and pulls it out: he holds between his fingers the bottle of Pernod.

Pedro, with his unbearable indiscretion, with his unforgivable absent-mindedness, lifts the bottle into the air and, as though pondering his bottle of aged red wine, he places it with the same storminess on top of the cabinet, behind the head of our great and cynical friend.

There is the cynic; I am facing him. The outline of his pointy, suspicious, bird-face, his newly balding head. Above his head, crowning it, like another bird perched on the head of the cynic, the Pernod.

And the cynic of Valdepinos swallows and talks, indifferent and undisturbed as he tells the story of a hysterical old woman we all know.

Twenty-four seconds! Pedro looks for his bottle of red wine, he finds it, holds it, feels it. Twenty-four seconds!

He stretches out his hand, grabs the Pernod. The Pernod disappears. He closes the cabinet . . . Good Lord! For twenty-four seconds—I repeat—the cynic's most cherished pleasure sat above and behind him. A shift of the eyes, and we would have drunk it to the last drop, and our ideas would have been different, our fortunes and our destiny would surely have been different.

In any case, this is certainly true for the cynic of Valdepinos.

But he had no idea. He didn't even suspect that for almost half a minute the sweet antidote to his Parisian nostalgia was ten or fifteen centimeters behind his head.

At this moment he is probably walking in solitary strides through a dark street. Poor Valdepinos!

As for me, I have returned to the seat I occupied during the meal. I have taken out the bottle of Pernod and returned it to where Pedro thoughtlessly left it.

The bottle of Pernod had been for the cynic of Valdepinos what I had been for the old man of the parchment papers. And the cynic of Valdepinos, moreover, had been for the bottle of Pernod what Estanislao Brun had been for the accident on the boulevard.

Nobody—neither man nor bottle—knew anything.

Except me.

Thus today, once again, I have gone against God.

August 1st

Today I lived a happy moment followed by a moment of grave concern.

Very early in the morning, the writer César Miró appeared in my study. He took a seat. And remained silent. Finally, he told me the following:

He had woken up in a good mood. He had jumped out of bed full of optimism. He had sat on the balcony, where his sense of happiness and optimism grew stronger: in the middle of the Plaza de Armas, he had seen his "Man dressed in green" speaking in a powerful voice, surrounded by public interest and enthusiasm. A good start to the day! Then he went back to bed and read the newspaper.

This was his happy moment and, through friendship, mine. But let's continue:

Miró lies peacefully once more in his bed with two arms at his side. Between them, the newspaper, spread open, and waiting to be read. But this is no time to read. He thinks about the spectacle in the plaza. Yes, let's think about it.

Soon the pages of the newspaper release a murmur, as if from the universe, which buzzes around the ears. He has to read. Miró lifts the newspaper up to his eyes, leaving it perpendicular to the surface of his still waters: his bed, his body, the floor, and the earth. He lifts the paper abruptly. He holds the paper, and looks at it. And here begins the second moment, the moment of grave concern:

As soon as he lifted the newspaper and brought it to the perpendicular position, every letter of every word on the first page, every one, without exception, came loose, detached itself from the newspaper, and fell with the quivering sound of a bell.

My dear friend! Alone in his room with a blank page before his eyes. My dear friend! Covered with thousands and thousands of meaningless, scattered letters.

And now the arduous task of putting them back in place, thousands and thousands of letters, one after another, until they come to signify what happened yesterday in all the corners of the world.

He picks up two I's, which must, without a doubt, belong to the words HIS HIGHNESS, who just got married. Progress! But they might also belong to RIBERI, who committed suicide.

He picks up an H and he picks up an E. There is not a newspaper that does not print each day on its front page the words His Excellence, which is abbreviated with the letters H. E. He continues, in this manner, down a safe path. But a doubt appears in his mind; has he made a profound error, for the H may have referred to the Holy sites that were desecrated last night; and the E could have referred to the Employers who on each continent quietly oppress their workers.

What difficult work: so fraught with dangers this interminable task of adjusting each fallen letter to recreate the word that brought them to life.

Better to abandon this mess and seek the advice of a friend.

Miró walks the length of my desk. At each step a letter untangles from his clothes. By my shoes there is an F; a T hangs from the bars on the window; an O bounces off the floor, rolls around and collides with an insect calmly bathing in the triangle of sun that visits my study at 9 o'clock each morning.

I can not find any advice to give him.

He leaves my house.

As he crosses the threshold, he drops a lower-case i, a pathetic i from some lost word that at one moment had an actual meaning. There it stands, erect, balancing its little dot.

As long as I shall live in this house, I will take care to not step on this i. And I will always turn to salute it. And it will stay in my doorway, like a guard who keeps my domestic worries from leaving the house, and who keeps the outside world from entering.

September 1st

Today I have come to the coast. So many of God's fingers, so many grave concerns led me to leave the city and search for equilibrium by the ocean.

I have sat on some rocks: the waves at my feet, and all that the poets sing of.

I have watched one of these waves for a period of an hour or more. It inflated, slipped, exploded, and dissolved . . . But the way it returned, always in the same form, it was always the same, throughout the entire hour or more, throughout all of the past, and most likely into the future as well.

Having made this discovery, and with an unshakable faith in it, I set out to ponder other thoughts, but before doing so I measured, and precisely demarcated the size of the unique wave, as we so spontaneously do in order to continue our meditations, in front of a tree, an animal, a colleague, or whatever thing that comes before our eyes and asks to be understood.

On this task I spent more than an hour, perhaps two, perhaps three. And the result was that I did not measure or demarcate anything. Because:

The wave comes in hidden beneath its own spine. It comes in with a long and sordid convulsion. Without a doubt, it hides its head, it sinks its head downwards, not wanting to expose itself to the breeze, to the sun, to the sky and the birds. It thinks only of the ocean's depths. And I only see the pain of its uncovered spine.

That was it. There was a vast pain in front of my eyes. But I could not clearly see a definite body to measure. This pain would stay in darkness, in smoke, disorienting spectators across the world.

The wave. The wave is one, one solitary entity. It is one, absolute in its existence. This solitary entity is what suffers. It doesn't matter that it dissolves. It remakes itself. It remakes itself thousands of times because its pain continues.

Fine. But let's rigorously demarcate the suffering body. This body which advances, undulates, thickens, and howls.

Now it twists, edges into white, curves, thunders. Thousands of specks of foam jump. The flowers behind it tremble. The sun in front of it shivers. A man stops. A dog barks. White specks jump across the entire sky. And at my side, here at my feet, in a narrow ridge of wet rocks, a trail of water, agile as a lizard, moves slowly, climbing, licking . . . It stops, and returns, snaps towards the solitary wave.

We measure.

The solitary wave, like an octopus, has extended its tentacles. One of those tentacles has come all the way to me. This sibilant water is always the wave; it is within its limits and demarcation. Proof of this is that it re-gathers near the body.

Once more it stretches. Better said, it stretches out a tentacle. It comes. Sprinkles. It stops three meters from my post. It reaches a small puddle where it plunges for a moment, touches, feels, pokes. It must pick up grains of salty, violet patina. It must feel a sweet, velvety pleasure as it pricks the moist and perfumed puddle with its tip.

The puddle has two concavities. The first one is big, the second one is smaller. Both are practically circular. They nearly form a stretched out 8, the bottom pointing towards the sea; the head towards the mountains.

The water rolls around inside. It dives into the first section, it searches every nook, it explores every last crack. It touches the joining neck. It examines the neck, quickly, and with certainty. It continues. It springs forward. It fills the second concavity. The solitary wave, submerged now in the ocean, experiences a healthy, salty pleasure, a pleasure repeated a thousand times throughout this vast camp of rocks and crossroads.

Fine. I am only responsible for this final bit that's next to me.

The water inside the 8-puddle now tries to retreat. The water in the small concavity is looking for an entry into the larger one. Once more it stirs around. Each drop of water wants to be the first to pass into the neck. No drop wants to remain still during the interval between the two movements. The entire small puddle fights, moves, intensifies, cries out for the vast sea from which it came. This homesick water completely enters the blue line of the deep horizon.

And I, from my post, observe the limited and disturbed life of the water in the second puddle.

It lives. It completes its task. It arrives, takes off, arrives. As I have said: homesick.

Therefore, it is not the wave. It is a separate entity, an independent unity . . . Thus?

The end of the large monster has to be marked as the neck of the 8. Its head, which looks out at the mountains, has become independent, has individualized. Throughout all of this immense being lived another smaller being, a being confused in its immensity, but which conquers the personality, and sharpens its instincts, if only in between rocks.

To measure the neck . . . But the body of the 8 lives the same life. The same phases, the same tragedy. And not only is there a similarity between the entire stream of water and a lizard: but there is as much life here as in the lizard as well.

Ok, then. I followed that trail until it finally fell into the ocean.

I glanced at the front of the wave at the moment it broke. A few minutes of contemplating the small puddle completely changed the panorama of the waters.

Each section of the waters, each piece in the wave, lived on its own. There was an isolated being in each section covered by my eyes, in each focal point, with its own purpose and passions, in the midst of millions of others, running along a parallel destiny . . . parallel, but nothing more. Thus the solitary wave, as an individual entity in its monstrous enormity, did not exist. It stood alone as an aggregate of different destinies bound together by a supreme design: an immaterial design with no body, with no head, no submerged head, no painful spine brushing the air.

The solitary wave was nothing more than a collective movement. A movement, a purpose, an abstraction.

Living as matter, as body, as nerves, with each circle drawn individually over the whole by the rays of my eyes. Like the spout that shoots white foam straight up to the sky, where it splits into fireworks. Here in my vision there has been no focal point; I have followed from bottom to top, and sung like a bird. And precisely above, where both water and vision have come to a halt, hundreds of points of water in hundreds of directions have at the same time individualized, and they have created, in the long meters of water, their global destiny, which bends them.

I can do nothing but stop with each drop. Each drop is the only personal living reality, like me, and like all the isolated men and beasts who live and suffer, alone, with one destiny and only one world inside their body.

Nothing but these drops, nothing else, because my eyes are not made to divide the world beyond.

My eyes stop there. There I stop. Until I begin again—drops of water, solitary wave, puddles, foam—leaning over the silence of a microscope.

Better to continue inversely. Measure on a large scale, sliding over the enormous spine.

That's how I have done it.

I have proceeded like a tube opened at each end which has spread to the infinity of the ocean. No more small individual beings pulsing in a common movement: now, moving parts, members, from one larger being which grows, becomes giant as my imagination navigates above the horizon. But I have not focused my eyes on any one part so as not to awaken and make dance the millions of tiny individuals that would jump around in the larger being as they came into my sight.

I have stayed well away from it, to the point where I have been forced to look at the sky: five wild ducks fly past in a triangle.

It is preferable to come to terms with ducks—even if there are five of them—than with raging waves. Man occupies in size, more or less, the midpoint between an atom and a star; therefore we are more or less the same in relation to the infinitely large or the infinitely small. But in size, and in all other ways, we are much closer to the duck than to the ocean. Therefore, there is no reason to take a position in relation to the latter when the former passes before your eyes.

Proof of this is that if a pain were to come from the ducks—as it comes from the waters—my size could right away verify the size and location of the one who feels it. The duck! There it goes! I can precisely measure the life of a flying duck. Each flap of its wings strikes me. But with him are four other ducks. I bring them together in my line of vision. My focal point is not one, but rather the triangle that cuts through the air. The life of each duck fades into the life of the triangle. And if I could place myself above, high above, so that I could see hundreds of groups of ducks flying and evolving, each small triangle would also fade with life and everything else, and the collection of all the ducks would look uniquely alive and vital, a unified beast, a unified life and purpose. And each group—which is to say, each bird!—one member, one pulsing cell, like the globules in our blood and in our entire body.

Higher! We must always elevate ourselves more!

All of these slippery stains formed beneath us by tiny black points, they are no longer the enormous solitary beast, but rather they are the life and substance of what now will be this entire stretch of coast and sea—the region beneath my eyes—pulsating, feeling, boiling.

And even higher? Perhaps the entire Earth would appear as one living reality. And my duck?

It passes by. There it goes. But it has dissolved between my fingers.

I have now started to jump along the rocks. As I move I am trying once again not to fix my eyes on anything so that the world will not multiply or increasingly unify. I have moved nervously through all that surrounds me, especially the ducks who I knew were passing above my head. I have gone on, feeling the urgent need to peacefully meditate on oceans, waves, puddles, and ducks, and to be able through my meditations to focus clearly on the point from where each independent life originates, or to discover that there is no such point.

Fine. Here in this cove there is peace. Sit, and let's meditate.

No more than a meter into my meditations, I see, standing in front of me, the same plump man who interrogated me with his eyes when I had tried to read the *Quixote*.

I will explain everything to him.

—Sir . . . (In a circular instance I explain to him all that I had contemplated).

I skip over a moment full of dubious rocks.

—Sir . . . (And at this point, as my meditations had already been verified, I tell him with a richness of detail and elegance without par, the results I had obtained. The plump man warmly congratulates me.)

Yes, but there is the moment on the rocks: an obligatory moment in the story. The first part is a direct observation of nature; the other, a silent meditation. And between the two, their union, a conduit that unifies them: the moment the observation asked to be meditated upon.

This moment—which in reality was accompanied by jumps on the rocks—I have to mention it to my audience. I have to mention it in some way. Let's see how:

—Sir, then . . . (There has to be a "then." How can it be avoided?) Then . . . I began to meditate . . . then . . . I thought . . .

No. It's best not to meditate or think if to do so we have to go through this.

Let's change the "then;" this could be the cause of it all.

—In the presence of this scene, sir . . . I could not keep myself from saying . . . I reflected in this way . . . and pondered as such . . .

Worse, worse. It looks like the problem is not in the "then" nor in the "in the presence of the scene." Could it be in the meditate, think, say, reflect, ponder?

The gap between the two moments bristled the rocks. It's like a tax that must be paid in order to obtain the necessary permission to elucidate our lucubrations. If there is something clear to extract from what is observed, then I must pass through a guardian-phrase to arrive. Bad, bad! Is there not some other way, a hidden path, a detour that evades the rocks? An obligation to pay our old friend "literature" with a little phrase entirely to her liking?

I am creating it; better said, I continue to create it. Because I created it, to be sure, in the peaceful cove. I created it and, in the presence of this creation, I did not meditate at all, not even a hundredth of a meditation, not on oceans, nor on waves, nor on puddles, nor ducks, nor on lives as large as constellations or as small as microbes.

October 1st

Today I returned to the edge of the sea. I have discovered a wonderful place. To get an idea of it, imagine a rock in the form of a monolith some 30-35 meters high; place it with the waves, in such a way that they smack its base; tint with blue sky all that is not smacked; now imagine a second rock of equal size and form; put it next to the first rock, with no more than two or three meters between them; proceed with this rock in the same way with respect to the waves and sky; cover the space between the two rocks with sand and seashells; sit sea birds at the top of the rocks; throw crabs and mussels at the bottom; surround the rocks with luche and cochayuyo leaves; heat the rocks in the sun and meditate upon the whole scene, enraptured in admiration.

This is what I have done from 4 o'clock in the afternoon until 5:10. At this time, I was struck by a sudden desire: to go between the two tall monoliths, to enter the sea. Five minutes of reflection, and forward!

Nothing interesting about my walk; nothing as well as I passed between the two rocks; but one small interesting detail as I attempted to enter the sea. Here it is:

As I stretched out my foot to kick the end of a wave transparently dying on the sand, the water retreated and my foot struck dry ground. Another step: the same thing. And another: the same. After seven steps, I stood still, hoping that a wave would once again emerge out of the undercurrent of the previous wave. I saw it form in the distance, I saw it come. As it came, I took another step and the same scene repeated itself. Ninth step, tenth . . . the same thing. Before the thirteenth attempt, I once again stood still. I only had one step left. You already know my feelings about the number 14.

Another wave came, the last! I burned my last step. The wave trickled away and once more I struck dry land.

Thus, with no more steps left, I buried myself up to my knees in the sand, and waited.

One minute, two minutes, three, four . . . Fourteen minutes, 14!

I heard in the air a solemn canticle: trumpets, bongos, cymbals, a bass drum, and a banjo. And the sea like me stood still during those fourteen minutes, and when it heard the canticle, it awoke and rolled away.

From each side, from all four cardinal points, it moved entirely towards one point on the horizon, before my eyes. And as it moved, it discovered, in my presence, its wet and scented hidden depths.

Watery plants with branches like the tongues of monsters stretched forward and then, when they could no longer feel the soft pressure of the sea, they exploded in aromas of iodine and salt. Thousands of creatures like spiders and as big as dogs went wild, running, smashing, and, as they discovered that there was no remedy to cure this illness, they buried their heads in the rocks and died a sweet death. Millions of fish rolled their astonished eyes; they emitted a groan, and dissolved into gelatin. And the underwater rocks, suddenly finding themselves naked in the sun, sunk into the ground, one by one, so as to never appear again. And the entire sea, from all sides—I repeat—continued to escape towards that one point, forming, as it traveled, an immense globe of water.

A pause. All the plants had exploded, all the creatures had died, all the fish had turned into a gelatin; not even a stone beneath the sun.

Then the sea transformed its sphere over the horizon into a curtain that covered the sky and hid the light.

Another pause. The curtain moved up and towards the coast. What a spectacular sight!

I think it's difficult for anyone to imagine this without having seen it with their own eyes. A sea, an ocean in place of the sky, ripples of foam in place of clouds, and a few displaced fish instead of seagulls and gannets. A spectacular sight! Beneath it, I was in ecstasy. The mussels swiftly opened and closed their shells, applauding like castanets; the crabs whistled like sirens from both ends of their shells; and the sea urchins allowed each shrimp to climb through their openings, where they stuck out their pincers and pointed them towards the enormous curtain that passed above our heads.

Suddenly, high up above, I noticed a red point. I fixed my eyes on it. The sea urchins, mussels, and crabs hid. The red point was falling. It was falling, and growing. It wasn't a point. It was a knot of branches, of arms. It was falling. It was going to land behind me.

It fell past the first hills behind me.

It took only a second to dig out my knees; my feet, another second. And I started to run.

What had fallen was a mass of coral. I sat near it, and this was what I observed:

As soon as it hit the ground, this mass consulted each of its individual entities, and they unanimously agreed to hold a vote of protest against all the zoophytes in the entire globe, and to intone a song in homage to the reign of the plant kingdom. The mass in question then grew larger and released into the air hundreds of intertwined branches, solid, shiny branches in a thousand varieties of red on white zigzags with fanciful trimmings. This is what it looked like from the ground up.

From the ground down it released sharp pointy roots. I directed a beam of vision at one of these roots and with it I began to descend, and I descended.

We passed through six different layers of earth at an outrageous speed, and when we arrived at the seventh, we stopped. The roots took a seat and asked permission to extract its nutrients. A character with a Mephistophelian face gave them all the permissions they desired. I then went back up along with the first nutritive ration.

I sat down, once again, in the same place and stared with astonishment at this coral tree. But something distracted me: standing beneath the tree, smiling, in a wide overcoat, a bowler hat, and with an open umbrella, was my old acquaintance: the plump man. He greeted me with the utmost courtesy, winked his eye and in a slow voice, said:

—Good afternoon.

He coughed, smiled, spat, and said:

—My name is Desiderio Longotoma.

He closed his umbrella, and continued:

—My good sir: I have the pleasure of telling you that with one eye I followed the depths of your vision while with the other eye I observed you during the entire period of your ascension and descension.

In regards to the former, I have nothing to tell you, for you saw as much as I, although I doubt that you have understood in all their breadth the different layers of our planet, above all, the seventh. But in regards to the latter, I should inform you of the following:

Through the duration of your voyage—it is more accurate to say the voyage of your vision—you slept with your other eye, and in the rest of your organism you experienced a sweet and beautiful dream. The ineffable imbecility of your expression, and the consummate cretinousness of your smile kept me from entertaining even the slightest doubts about the nature of your aforementioned dream.

I do not want, thus, to be at all ambiguous when I assure you that you believed with all certainty in a heavenly region that contained all that is good, noble, and beautiful in this world.

Nor do I wish to remain in the terrain of falsehood when I assure you that as your vision traveled through the first six layers, and especially as it spent the night in the seventh, you observed with distraction and disdain, and thus you could not refrain from—human nature, of course—comparing the sweetness of paradise with this layer's Mephistophelian character and rotten decay, and concluding that you preferred the former one thousand and one times more than the latter.

It is extremely painful for me to refute your convictions in this respect, especially since they are so firmly rooted in your brain. But since I have been sent here to clarify your thinking, I must proceed by extracting from the center your fixed convictions and reestablishing balance and truth by taking what is at the top and putting it at the bottom, and putting at the bottom what is at the top.

Without wasting any time, now that time is pressing, I must tell you that you are correct, in every sense of the word correct, to have classified as Mephistophelian and demonic the beings and objects in the seventh layer, and as pure and celestial all that you observed when you closed your eyes and entered the heavenly vault. But I also must advise you—and I request that you give this all of your attention—that it is an incredible and unspeakable human error, which has occurred for centuries and centuries, to attribute an ominous tint to the subterranean beings in the seventh layer, and a benevolent tint to those beings who shine in the blue of the upper layer.

An error, good sir, a profound error!

In the course of the past century, hundreds, perhaps thousands of magicians have vigorously fought to create this ridiculous change of values, and they have been so successful that it can now be said, without exaggeration, that there is not a human being on Earth who does not believe that evil exists in those creatures with horns, tails, pointy eyebrows, who smell of sulphur, and who carry sharp swords; and that good exists in what is blue, in what emits the fragrance of lilies, in what glows like quivering candles, in what gently lowers its eyelids.

My good sir, I repeat: an error, a profound error!

It is exactly the opposite.

Centuries ago, evil was seen in white petals, soft silk, and the gentle trill of the night air. I request that you blindly believe me. And I request, as well, that you blindly believe that neither one way of thinking nor the other is definitive: they are only paths, long and tortuous paths that in the end arrive only at themselves.

And since I undoubtedly know, dear sir, that your heart's deepest desire is to go towards what is good, it pleases me greatly to inform you of the best possibilities to attain this good.

This tormented coral tree that takes in nutrients from the seventh layer of demons and vermin, throws, as you see, a great red shadow, which reflects all that is created and accomplished in this layer. Sit in this shadow, and when you feel that you have been inundated by its influence, contemplate, with both body and soul, your deepest thoughts, and perhaps one day you will see for yourself what is good. For not one human being has been able to meditate on this good without having first spent several years sitting in a similar shadow, or under the influence of something analogous.

I hope that you will be able to take the utmost advantage of the wise advice that I, your most faithful and revered servant and friend, have given to you. I look forward to seeing you again.

And my name, I repeat, is Desiderio Longotoma.

That said, he finished his good-byes, opened his umbrella, and left.

And now I sit, beneath this tormented and magnificent tree, and meditate on his wise words.

November 1st

Today I had surgery on my ear and telephone. Doctor Hualañé, in person, administered the chloroform and scalpel.

This is how the events took place:

For quite some time I have loved Camila, wildly. She loves me one day out of every eight, and during the remaining days she laughs at me, wildly, and there is as much wildness in her laughter as there is in my love.

For the past seventeen days, however, Camila's laughter has gone beyond all previous wildness to the point where today I returned to my house with a greater desire to die than to live. But before putting an end to my existence, I dialed her telephone number[3] and listened.

A few seconds later, Camila spoke. By the tone of her voice, I thought that this perhaps was the one day out of every eight. But then I experienced a cruel deception. I said:

—I love you, Camila! Camila, I love you! She responded with a quick little laugh, a sharp laugh, which jabbed into me like the sting of a rattlesnake.

—My Camila, have mercy—I shouted three times.

And her laughter only grew louder.

Overcome with anger, I tried with an abrupt and decisive gesture to yank the receiver from my ear, and to decisively cut off all communication between us. But just as I began this gesture, I felt a strong pain throughout my ear, as though it were being pulled by thousands of demons. At the same time, her laughter continued to pierce me with a sharpness that bristled my nerves.

—Camila, I beg you, stop laughing.

In vain. Her laughter now echoed interminably.

—Camila, it would be better if you told me you hated me.

Nothing. I tried once more to remove the receiver from my ear. It resisted in such a way that I understood that if I kept trying I would knock over the base to which it was mounted. I tried to pull it away with a gentle touch. Useless. I tried to unscrew it like a bolt. Also useless. And her inexhaustible laughter kept pouring out, and spreading across my head. What could I do?

There was only one thing to do: reach for the scissors to cut the cord. I didn't care if the phone was stuck to my ear as long as I didn't have to hear her cold and scornful laughter.

---

3. Camila's telephone number is 52061, or rather: 5+2+0+6+1=14!

I gave the cord a snip and split it in two. Salvation!

But no! Her loud and copious laughter kept coming.

I ran through the house. Sweet remedy!

Silence. As soon as I was a few meters from the phone, silence.

What a relief! I would no longer be tortured by that diabolical laughter which evokes all the unhappiness Camila sees in me. No longer would that symbol of my unfortunate love continue to enter in through my auditory nerve. Silence, silence. But soon I began to notice that, in truth, there was too much silence.

Not even a whisper, or a murmur, or a muffled echo, nothing. My feet on the floorboards stepped on cotton; when I clapped my hands, not even one wave of sound was released into the air; when I screamed at the top of my lungs, my voice was an underground vault. Complete silence.

Terrified, I picked up a bottle of wine from the Rhine Valley and threw it against the bathroom mirror: the bottle shattered, the wine flew through the air, and the mirror was pulverized. All of this in the silence of a cloudless night over a snowy and deserted mountaintop. The peace of a tomb, an absolute peace. A perfect suppression of any manifestation of all auricular life.

I won't deny it: I turned pale as this black cloak fell over me, isolating me from the side of existence on which all other human beings live.

Nevertheless, a hope. With cautious steps, I walked towards the room with the telephone. Silence, an ever-present silence.

I arrived. I stopped three meters from the phone, and leaned against the wall. Each minute a drop of blood dripped from the severed phone cord. But not a sound nor a whisper, nothing.

I walked no faster than the minute hand on the clock. Silence.

Silence, yes, throughout the entire interminable first meter.

Until I arrived at the very beginning of the second meter.

Then, from far away, at an extraordinary distance, I heard, faintly but at the same time with clarity, a jingling, which, because of its distance, made me think of antipodes; it sounded like crystal shards on ice.

I kept walking. The jingling grew louder. Now it sounded like a voice draining the house, soaking it. One more step: the jingle changes, takes shape, vibrates, bounces off the walls. My destiny is marked: defenseless, subdued,

I take the last step. And I am nearly deafened by the wounding sound of Camila's sarcastic laughter.

No more precaution, no more deliberation. I jump from one side to the other: towards the telephone, away from it; towards the piercing laughter, then towards the absolute silence . . . O the incessant scorn from my one and only love, o the silent abyss between myself and the world.

And the days begin to pass, outside of my eardrums.

Monotonous days, exactly the same.

I sleep well, and I wake up at the same time as always, but I feel three times more tired than before, now that one of the three ways of sleeping is no longer available to me: I can sleep on my back, and on one side, but the telephone receiver stuck to my ear prevents me from sleeping on the other.

I get dressed and look at myself for several minutes in front of the remaining pieces of my broken mirror. I test out all the possible methods of taking the phone off my ear: force, subtlety, a knife, a lubricant. No success.

I walk with soft steps through each room of the house and, from time to time, I entertain myself—the only entertainment possible—by verifying and re-verifying—until I am properly sated—that everything becomes silent in my presence.

I then walk to the telephone, always with the naïve and distant hope that silence will have penetrated its domain. No! Camila's laughter is always there, entrenched in the machine, and suspended in several meters of the surrounding air.

I return to my study. I put a record on the phonograph and, as always, I comfortably settle into my armchair. Each day, I like to experience the great pleasure—unavailable to others—of knowing that in the entire room there is sound, even when I don't hear a thing.

I stretch out on my bed. I close my eyes, and meditate, and on each occasion—like clouds of smoke taking shape, or like small shapes swimming in the clouds—I sense that another interpretation of the silent world is beginning to form, an interpretation useless to anyone who can hear. Another face, another meaning, another reason, which only begins to form when the silence is definitive unto eternity.

But then I remember that for me this isn't the case. For if on one side I do not hear, I hear—and do I hear!—the moment my receiver enters the zone occupied by Camila's laughter.

Maybe this time there will be silence?

My hope is revived, a double hope: no longer to hear her wretched laughter; and to walk unblemished through my new perceptions of this insinuated world.

I run to the telephone. I extend my neck. And tilt the receiver.

Camila laughs, Camila laughs, jingles and drives ice and nails into my lacerated heart.

And the entire scene repeats itself. The phonograph spins another record.

It's like this every day, every hour. Either the tomb, or the scorn of Camila.

Slowly the habit possessed me. My entire organism adapted to this new mode of existence. The tomb filled with silent meanings; the laughter infiltrated me with the pleasure of suffering. A sweet and sorrowful happiness came more and more to take the place of my previous activities. Thousands of objects which hid from my intimate life beneath the ever-echoing sounds of existence now obediently presented themselves to me like delicate gifts. All the empty space that surrounded me became populated with unsuspected existences. And over this new world, the suffocating pleasure of torment that Camilla inflicted upon me absorbed like pepper in my flesh.

It's been three days since I told myself that, from this point on, I will be happy until the end of my life. But yesterday, doctor Hualañé appeared at my door.

The good man had been informed—I will not discuss how—of what he—and up until recently, I—considered to be my disgrace. I told him there was no disgrace. But he wouldn't listen to me. He went to the window and opened it wide. With thousands of faces and gestures, he led me to understand that the entire outside world, all that could be seen of the city, the distant mountains, and the sky, was infinitely flowing with living sounds.

The good man tempted me. He has tempted me. I tilted my head.

Today he has come; he has operated on me, and chloroformed me. Afterwards, he reconnected the receiver to the bloody, hanging cord. And today I once again heard the sounds of life.

And all of the unsuspected existences, and all of my peaceful meditations have vanished. And all of the pleasure in pain has disappeared. Now everything echoes frantically. And so to know what to expect in this world which provokes in me an infernal chaos, I have no choice but to pick up the phone and dial 52061, and wait.

December 1st

Today I returned from a long trip. A few days after the operation, and at the advice of Doctor Hualañé, I boarded in Valparaiso the *S.S. Orangutan* of the H. T. T. K. C.

We stopped at the following ports:

Coquimbo.—A cheerful and picturesque town in the middle of a large and peaceful bay. Coquimbo is known as the land of coconut and cherry trees. Everything here is born, grows, lives, fructifies, and dies in accordance with the cherry and coconut trees. What does not follow this line is immediately picked up by the police and thrown into the sea with a stone tied to its neck, and if it does not have a neck, then the stone is tied to its most prominent part. During our stay we had occasion to see two definitive submersions: a) a German scholar who had the nerve to declare in front of the country's elite that the study of extra-sclerotic orbital pterygoidal worms was more important than the study of any coconut or cherry tree regardless of how many of them there were in Coquimbo; and b) a mattress which had innocently torn a bit of its fabric, and exposed its contents to the eyes of the authorities: cotton stuffing, and not the coconut filament or cherry sawdust found in all the other mattresses of the city.

Aside from those acts which offended our sensibilities as Santiaguinos, the rest of our stay in Coquimbo was wonderful, absolutely wonderful.

Wherever we looked and in any way that we looked, our eyes fell on a coconut tree guarded by two cherry trees, and the only variation to this ineffable scene was the rare occasion on which there was one cherry tree guarded by two coconut trees.

In fact our enchantment with Coquimbo became so unbearable that the Captain decided to set sail without any further delay.

Antofagasta.—A cheerful and picturesque town in the middle of a large and peaceful bay. A city that has left us with inerasable memories—for a city entirely of wool offers great surprises for the traveler. Wool houses, wool streets, wool trees, and wool people. And from time to time, a famished fakir, entangled in wool, comes to the city, and yawns.

So much peace in that woolen sky. The residents of Antofagasta contemplate the sky by raising their woolen pupils. They subtly alter the name of their beloved "An-to-fa-ga-sta," and fall into ecstasy at the thought of how in the past, everything—because it was not made of wool—deteriorated, and how now—now that everything is made of wool—nothing deteriorates. Then they tune all of the instruments in the region to the key of F, and with these instruments—always in F—they sing, swaying until the sun sets in the west, leaving in its place the taste of astronomical wool.

Iquique.—A cheerful and picturesque town in the middle of a large and peaceful bay. But how different it is from the previous two cities, almost as though it did not belong in the same country! You see:

Iquique is the cradle, the universal cradle, of all the birds in the world whose song is shrill and hesitant.

Any bird that sings like this, and who did not see the light of day in this land will not survive: it will surely be eaten by serpents, scorpions, tarantulas, and other bacteria. The birds, in contrast, that were born here—and who later take off in fast flight through the five parts of the globe—make it to old age, make it to a ripe old age, to that old age without feathers, without wings or beaks, though always with their exquisite song, their sharp and stunning song.

The people who live here try to imitate these notes. And with good reason. The sound they release into the air is so enchanting that ten minutes before anchoring all of the passengers aboard the *Orangutan* began to chirp like these pretty birds. When the captain heard us, he silenced our deafening whistles with the ship's siren, and then he gave orders to anchor.

Mollendo.— A cheerful and picturesque town in the middle of a large and peaceful bay. But this town is completely different.

In Mollendo, everything is round, cottony, and brown. And moreover everything is soft and cushy, so much so that its residents recline anywhere and everywhere, wherever they happen to feel drowsy: on a branch, on a rock, in a chimney, on the ocean's waves, absolutely anywhere.

Then they eat. The only thing they eat are earthy-tasting round rolls. Afterwards, they rinse their hands in the sea, and since the water is brown, and since the bread crumbs are also brown, with each rinse of the hands, Mollejo becomes more and more brown. And with the earthy wind that blows here every night, and with the lazy licks of the waves, Mollendo becomes more and more round.

The captain has told me that within a few years this entire place will be one round, cottony ball the color of *café con leche*.

Huacho.— A cheerful and picturesque town in the middle of a large and peaceful bay. It is also an extremely curious port. It is formed by mountains of transparent salt, just like those salty stones that are licked by cows. The sea, when it reflects these mountains, turns a glaucous color.

The people who live here—it goes without saying—are like people everywhere, except that when they cross these mountains they acquire strange forms, like frail little figures.

As the ship came to anchor, it left behind a trail of colorless, featureless spittle. We watched with dying eyes as glaucous as the sea.

Pacasmayo.— A cheerful and picturesque town in the middle of a large and peaceful bay. But what a difference from the previous towns! What a contrast! What crazy colors! Every imaginable color and many other colors which perhaps I could not see were in the leaves and the fruits of its trees. And each color was bright, vibrant, definitive. A crazed painter's jumbled palette stretched to the sea. Yes, the thick sea was like oil colors; it moved slowly, and it tinged the hull of the ship with a rainbow that detached itself as we traveled. The sailors would dip a finger in these colors, then suck on it happily. And the strangest thing about this curious port was that a parrot could be seen in each tree, in each branch, in each fruit.

All of the parrots screamed at the same time and without even one second of interruption. The noise was so loud that during the twenty hours of our stay we communicated through sign language because we could not hear a word.

As we sailed away, Pacasmayo looked like a giant blaze with fiery tongues of red, yellow, green, and orange, which moved and twisted as a bit of wind swayed the branches of the trees and the feathers of the parrots.

We heard from the blaze the bitter cry of the birds; and later we heard an out of tune murmur that lasted until the sun went down. Pacasmayo disappeared, and the parrots were silent.

Pimentel.— A cheerful and picturesque town in the middle of a large and peaceful bay. But quite different from the previous town.

A splendid Nile green plain, endless, with thousands, millions of trees, equidistant one to the other. Their trunks stood straight as pins; their leaves were round and almost black. The captain himself told me that these trees produced pepper. Once he said that, we both started to sneeze loudly.

During the three days we were anchored here, we saw nothing: not one dog on the street, nor one fish in the water, nor one bird in the air. Bored, the captain gave orders to lift anchor, and the *Orangutan* set sail.

Patia.— A cheerful and picturesque town in the middle of a large and peaceful bay. Enormous, low-hanging green leaves, which tilt towards the earth, forming blue hollows.

The people from Patia recline in the hollows, lazily humming a tune. They eat avocados with oil. They throw the rinds into the bright blue sea, which flows beneath the leaves. A sea that has no horizon, for where the horizon should appear, the leaves mask everything.

Out of curiosity, I picked up a leaf. I too could not see the horizon, but a mountain that hid the horizon appeared, and came closer and closer to me. A mountain that surrounded the entire sea. It was a metallic cherry red, exactly the color of an avocado pit. This cherry red was reflected in short though numerous rays on the bright blue water. The captain told me that the mountain was actually made of metal and that from its base it emitted and scattered liquid into the sea. In response to this, I let go of a leaf and once again the green saturated it. My response was completely useless.

Manta.— A cheerful and picturesque town in the middle of a large and peaceful bay.

This town has three inhabitants who rotate the responsibility of completing the three necessary activities in this land. While one person keeps guard, the second sleeps, and the third one eats. Afterwards, the one who keeps guard sleeps, the one who sleeps eats, and the one who eats keeps guard. And this, successively, until infinity.

The one who keeps guard sits atop a pine tree; he salutes the passing ships; he runs to greet those ships that anchor, and he shakes the hands of important officials, passengers, and the crew.

The one who sleeps lies in a red tent. He sleeps deeply, and dreams—always the same dream—unhappily, of the beauty and grandeur of Guayaquil.

The one who eats squats behind a bush. He sticks out his hand and grabs a gannet. He eats it alive, with its beak, its feet, its feathers, every part of it. The bird lets out blood-curdling cries.

In effect. Not even an hour after we anchored our ears were drilled with the most horrible, the most frightful howl that could come from any living being. We then saw how that scream scared the other birds in the area, especially the other gannets: the sky filled with hundreds of thousands of birds overcome with fear. And amongst them were the sad and serene brothers of the victim, majestically beating their wings, as bitter tears fell from their eyes.

One of these birds, distracted from its path by the smell, did not fly over the bay, but instead landed on the porthole of my cabin.

The voice of alarm instantaneously traveled from one end of the ship to the other.

—Gannet on board! Gannet on board!

The flag of danger was then raised atop the mizzenmast; from the foremast, the flag of resignation flew in the face of evil. And the siren cried lugubriously, as the two anchors, without having been hoisted by anyone, rose pitifully to the deck like two drenched old ladies.

The captain grew grave and sullen. His only words were:

—Return . . .

Creaking from its core, the *Orangutan* screeched off from the anchorage and sailed towards the horizon.

How sad it was to come so suddenly to the end of our trip! What a disappointment! And to think that we were only miles from our final destination, the port of Buenaventura, which, according to public opinion, is a cheerful and picturesque town in the middle of a large and peaceful bay.

But there was nothing to be done. The captain had said "return" and the *Orangutan* meekly obeyed.

Describing a wide circle in the ocean, we returned without docking at any ports. And today, with great joy, we saw once again atop its hills the cheerful and picturesque town of Valparaiso, whitening the middle of its large and peaceful bay.

I spent the days of our return locked in my cabin, lying on my bunk, without seeing anyone, without eating or moving a limb. Behind me, and above my head, sat the gannet of Manta, slowly flitting its wings. This was how I dreamed the dreams that came to me at sea, and how I happily filtered those distant memories that struck my mind, and how I colored in yellow and green those projects for next year that began to germinate and flutter to the rhythm of the ocean's waves.

And in this way, the noble bird accompanied me, day after day, hour after hour, without screaming, or even batting an eyelid, only flitting in silence his soft cotton wings.

And as I set foot on land, I watched the bird fly into the distance, then launch beak-first into the water behind a catfish, who swam slowly behind a sea flea.

And we never saw each other again.

December 31st

Today I slowly and carefully reread this diary. I have no doubts: it must be good for this very simple reason:

Each day begins with "Today I . . ." followed by a participle.

"Today I awoke, had, have, crossed, experienced, wandered, lived, came, returned, had, returned, reread."

And a diary whose every entry begins this way—I assure you—is touched by perfection, for it fulfills the inviolable law—the sacred law!—that has been promulgated by every young girl who has poured out her feelings with ink on paper, and by all the wise professors of grammar and rhetoric.

Amen.

CONTRIBUTORS

Juan Emar was the pen name of Álvaro Yáñez Bianchi (1893-1964). He was the son of an influential politician and diplomat, and he lived intermittently between Santiago and Paris. In Paris, and later in Chile, he was associated with surrealist groups, and he took the name Juan Emar because of its connection to the French phrase "J'en ai marre" (I'm fed up). Between 1935-1937, he published four books: *Miltín, Un año, Ayer* and *Diez*, which were largely ignored in Chile, as he managed to upset the dominant literary circles of his time. In the 1970s, and more recently, his work was reissued in Chile, and he is now thought of as one of the most important twentieth-century Chilean and South American fiction writers, a precursor to such writers as Julio Cortázar and Juan Rulfo.

Daniel Borzutzky is the author of two books: *The Ecstasy of Capitulation* (BlazeVox, 2007) and *Arbitrary Tales* (Triple Press, 2005). His translation of *Port Trakl* by Chilean poet Jaime Luis Huenún will be published by Action Books in late 2007. Daniel's own work has appeared in dozens of print and online journals. He lives in Chicago.

BOOK REVIEWS

JACQUES JOUET. *UNE MAUVAISE MAIRE*. PARIS: POL, 2007. 125. PP. 12 EUROS.

Jacques Jouet's new book is the latest addition to "The Novel Republic," an ambitious prose cycle currently numbering some fifteen volumes, in which he proposes to track the fleeting detail of daily life in contemporary France along a variety of vectors, personal, social, and political. Here, he focuses upon "Marie Basmati," the mayor of La Chapelle, a small municipality in the suburbs of Paris. She's a leftist and a member of the French Communist Party, but she is no simple apparatchik. Deeply committed to the loftiest democratic principles of the Republic, she feels that ideology must not be allowed to dictate the practical gestures involved in providing service to her constituency. In short, Marie is that rare bird in our social landscape, the sincere politician.

That in itself suffices, perhaps, to make her a "bad mayor," as the novel's title suggests, punning on the French homonyms maire and mère, "mayor" and "mother." Chief among her other sins is that she has a life apart from politics—though one senses that her private life is somewhat less engaging than in the past. Her husband, a recently-retired teacher, is more and more interested in global social issues and less and less interested in his wife. Her children have flown the nest toward universities, and return home on different terms. When Marie finds a young man of North African descent named Masmaïl one morning, naked and tied to a tree on the grounds of City Hall, she will begin to discover how things can go awry when the spheres of the political and the intimate collide.

That collision and others like it animate *Une Mauvaise Maire* from first page to last, as Jouet weaves various events into an intriguing narrative fabric wherein the utterly banal competes for our attention with the exceptional, much as it does in the texture of our daily lives. Indeed, Marie Basmati is undone neither by salacious scandal nor by Machiavellian political maneuvers, but rather by the price of meat. "It's the economy, stupid," as Bill Clinton famously suggested to Bush Senior: that's a notion which Jouet's economical tale brings home in fresh ways. This is a smart, tactful, amusing, strategically understated novel, one that bears lessons not only for the French Republic, but for others that one might care to imagine as well. — WARREN MOTTE

OLIVIER ROLIN. *PAPER TIGER*. TRANS. WILLIAM CLOONAN. UNIVERSITY OF NEBRASKA PRESS, 2007. 203 PP. PAPER: $17.95.

At the *Bal des Têtes*, where he finds his acquaintances aged almost beyond recognition, Proust's narrator takes decisive steps towards embracing memory as the subject of his as-yet-unwritten opus, and retreating from the empty conciliations of lived life. Concerned as it is with recapturing the past—in this case, the narrator's days as a militant Maoist revolutionary for "The Cause" in Paris during the '60s and '70s—Proust is a fitting genius loci for *Paper Tiger*, though here the tone is not one of celebration, however elegiac, for the power of memory and art, but of dissolution and defeat. Meeting the daughter of a dead comrade at a reunion held in a Paris bar, seeing the more or less bourgeois grotesques he and his old friends have become, Rolin's narrator, now a middle-aged "man of letters," begins a long monologue—half reverie, half come-on—about her father's life and death, and about life together in their cell of The Cause. Christening his car "Remember," and imagining it to be a spaceship traveling past the billboards and neon signs of the galaxy of Paris (shades of *Alphaville*), the narrator spirits his willing audience away, driving till dawn while spouting muddled anecdote after anecdote: stories of botched kidnappings and even attempted assassinations, peppered with allusions to a history and literature (classical and partisan both) that his passenger can't begin to follow. Rolin's first novel to appear in English is a remarkable, breathless flood of language: an attempt to outdistance the futility of memory—particularly that of an epoch and ideology that now seem, regretfully, to exist outside of time: co-opted and without consequence (a paper tiger)—with no other weapon than wit. Its melancholy is decisive: the narrator worries that the children of the present are incapable of understanding that there was a time when the world could have turned out differently, while fearing too that The Cause was never more than romantic idiocy and ill-informed fanaticism. In the end, "Remember" runs out of gas, and the narrator—and his audience—must return to an Earth that is clearly past its prime. — JEREMY M. DAVIES

ARNOST LUSTIG. *FIRE ON WATER: PORGESS AND THE ABYSS*. TRANS. ROMAN KOSTOVSKI (*PORGESS*) AND DEBORAH DURHAM-VICHR (*THE ABYSS*). NORTHWESTERN UNIVERSITY PRESS, 2006. 248 PP. $16.95.

After surviving three concentration camps, Arnost Lustig escaped en route to a fourth. Why he survived when so many died has remained a haunting obsession, as his considerable body of work attests. Survival makes and mars the career of Porgess, eponymous hero of his own tale, whose flight from certain death mimics that of his creator, to a point. Gunned down running from an eastbound train by a Nazi officer the day before Germany's surrender, his spine shattered, Porgess lives on, barely. In his bedroom he and the unnamed narrator muse over youthful feats and lost acquaintances, his visitor recalling Porgess's promise, his reckless attraction as "the most handsome boy in Jewish Prague," while the two trade thoughts on girls, jazz, and Porgess's fascination with numerology. A legacy of guilt in a world made strange by their unexplainable presence in it informs the two young men's touching mutual regard and alienation, spellbound by events from which neither can ever stop reeling. *The Abyss* into which David Wiesenthal, protagonist of the other short novel in this edition, tumbles during an avalanche, beyond reach of all but a hallucinogenic succession of dreams, becomes his procrustean bed. As in *Porgess*, the most arresting images emerge from David's recollection of heartbreaking incidents from the camps and their aftermath, particularly vignettes of tragic young women of his acquaintance, victims and shattered survivors, whose effect upon him mingles with semi-conscious fantasies to summon dream lovers of terrible potency. Snatches of conversation with his dead mother prepare David for the appearance of the woman for whom he has spent his whole life longing. Bewildered at the meaninglessness of postwar life, awaiting the dénouement to yet another twist of fate, David's wistful visions of women palliate his grievous burden, that chance alone spared him a doom befalling millions. — MICHAEL PINKER

INGEBORG BACHMANN. *LAST LIVING WORDS*. TRANS. LILIAN M. FRIEDBERG. GREEN INTEGER, 2005. PAPER: $14.95.

"We are in Vienna, more than ten years after the war. 'After the war'—that is the measure of our time." With this, relayed by the narrator in Bachmann's "Among Murderers and Madmen," one of the finest stories collected here, Bachmann situates the reader of *Last Living Words* accordingly. As an Austrian who grew up under Nazi rule and witnessed the unmasking of government-sanctioned genocide in her early adulthood, Bachmann dispatches from a society and culture in ruins with both compassion and art. Occasionally fascism's ghosts materialize in soldiers' tales and in the recollections of ex-government officials, but there is another quiet fascism found more often here, lurking in the marriage bed or drifting about the dinner table shared amongst friends. In her time, the influential Gruppe 47, a collective of post-war German writers, lauded Bachmann's work. She was awarded their prestigious prize in 1953, yet Bachmann was not content with settling in Germany and enjoying literary celebrity amidst this group of mostly male peers. Like her dear friend the poet Paul Celan, Bachmann chose a life of exile, eventually settling in Rome where she died in an apartment fire in 1973. The fiction collected here does not always live up to the standard set by her masterful experimental novel *Malina*, available to an English readership in a translation by Philip Boehm. However, *Last Living Words* is invaluable for illuminating the breadth of work published in Bachmann's lifetime and places her more firmly as a precursor to the gorgeous brutality of Elfriede Jelinek, and further reveals Bachmann as one of the great post-war German-language writers, one too seldom read and translated into English. — JOHN VINCLER

DONALD BRECKENRIDGE, ED. *THE BROOKLYN RAIL FICTION ANTHOLOGY*. HANGING LOOSE PRESS, 2006. 420 PP. PAPER: $24.00.

"I am tempted to say this is how love works, burying everyone in the same style," confesses the narrator in Diane Williams's opening story of *The Brooklyn Rail Fiction Anthology*. The same accusation is often made of anthologies, which are essentially tastemakers. *The Brooklyn Rail* is a tastemaker of a unique kind; the free, not-for-profit newspaper based in Brooklyn, NY describes its political, arts, and literature coverage as: "slanted opinions, artfully delivered" with a "real commitment . . . less to a program than a place, or better yet, to a set of traditions that place represents." This lack of allegiance to a distinct aesthetic makes Donald Breckenridge's offering an eclectic mix of often original and sophisticated writing. In many ways, this collection represents not only the *Rail* but also contemporary Brooklyn more broadly: inventive, adventurous, and sometimes a bit smug. Nonetheless, these authors and their subjects are not limited to a specific borough or even generation. Included are distinguished names such as Brian Evenson, Susan Daitch, Jonathan Baumbach, Leslie Scalapino, and Albert Mobilio, and welcome new translations of Robert Pinget and Carmen Firan. Many of these brief stories are self-aware first-person narratives, yet they vary stylistically, comprising the quirky (John Reed interviews Mickey Mouse), the formally innovative (Johannah Rodgers crafts an elegant narrative sestina), the disturbing (Lynda Schor imagines her young daughter as a high-end hooker), and the humorously self-deprecating (Jacques Roubaud defends his poetry to a group of schoolchildren; Michael Martone learns his Harvard students are the interns receiving his manuscripts at *The Atlantic Monthly*). Breckenridge's deft assembly has an intricate and almost novelistic trajectory, providing an engaging journey through twenty-first century dysfunctional relationships and the challenges of career and identity in an untidy world. Such an achievement marks an impressive moment for the *Rail*; it also stands on its own as an invaluable collection of both well-known avant-garde voices and exciting emerging talent. — STEFANIE SOBELLE

DANIELLE DUTTON. *ATTEMPTS AT A LIFE*. TARPAULIN SKY PRESS, 2007. 78 PP. PAPER: $14.00.

In one of the prose pieces in Danielle Dutton's first collection, the author uses a text from Céline reproduced on a collage given to her by a friend, a fittingly personal history for her relationship to these words given her project at hand. Collage is the operating formal device utilized throughout the slim volume, where the author repurposes and recontextualizes lines from writers such as Ann Quin, Robert Walser, Katherine Mansfield, Sappho, even from Jerome Rothenberg's anthology *Revolution of the Word*. With this project, and her attempt to breathe new life into these originary works, Dutton seems to be carrying through Borges' saying that he was more proud of what he has read than what he has written. Jackson MacLow made famous the technique of borrowing from and reappropriating literary texts with his poems that used what he called a "diastic" or "spelling-thru" method with Virginia Woolf's *The Waves*. Except for a brief list at the end, the reader of *Attempts at a Life* is not told how exactly Dutton performs surgery on the source texts. The stories often read like curious abstract puzzles, and one should resist running to the bookshelves to attempt to break the code. The best pieces call to mind that of Gertrude Stein or Diane Williams, both obvious influences on Dutton whose lines she also pastiches, with a voice that comes off as refreshingly eccentric, as in the title story, a collection of nine fragmented first-person biographies. She also reimagines the lives of famous heroines from literature, from Hester Prynne to Virginia Woolf's Mary Carmichael in *A Room of One's Own* to Alice James to Madame Bovary. Her glorious version of *Jane Eyre* reads like one of *The Guardian*'s congested reads as reimagined by Gertrude Stein or Jane Bowles. — KATE ZAMBRENO

W. C. BAMBERGER, ED. *SELECTED LETTERS: GUY DAVENPORT AND JAMES LAUGHLIN*. W. W. NORTON & CO., 2007. 262 PP. $29.95.

This is the seventh volume of selected letters from the archive of James Laughlin, former editor of New Directions. Davenport and he exchanged letters briefly in the 1970s, but their correspondence became regular from

1983 through 1997. Although Davenport opened every letter with "Dear Mr. Laughlin", the two men exchanged frank details about their writings. The starting point for their friendship was a shared interest in Thomas Merton and Ezra Pound; Davenport was exploring the publication of the later Cantos and Laughlin brought out his study *Pound Az Wuz* in 1987. In this period Laughlin was gradually giving up publishing responsibilities and concentrating instead on his own writing. Davenport gave particular praise to the latter's 1994 collection *9 Ridge Road*, named after Laughlin's address in Rutherford, NJ. Apart from the wealth of detail in this selection about both writers' publications and Davenport's paintings, the letters shed rather more light on Davenport's work, especially as he tended to be reticent about making his sentiments public. Thus, he explains that a breakthrough in his work came when he realized: "I mustn't write about anything from my own experience . . . but to work with my own imagination." Undoubtedly painting had its impact on Davenport's descriptions because at first he attempted an objectivist method of externalities ("the man got off the bus," as he puts it). The two writers shared the excitement of exchanging and discussing ideas, although Davenport seems to have been the more pessimistic about the life of the mind: "I think we've entered the Intellectual Ice Age," he declared in 1988. Nor was his view of modern art any better: in 1994 he wrote: "What's passing for art now is daubs and piles of rocks." Both writers were clearly coming to the end of their careers, but their letters show no signs of them losing their intellectual vigor. — DAVID SEED

ROBERT ELSIE, ED. *BALKAN BEAUTY, BALKAN BLOOD: MODERN ALBANIAN SHORT STORIES*. TRANS. ROBERT ELSIE AND JOHN HODGSON. NORTHWESTERN UNIVERSITY PRESS, 2006. 160 PP. $16.95.

Albanian literature *per se* dates from the twentieth century, largely a consequence of political repression. Elsie's anthology, the first to bring Albanian writers to readers of English, displays the conflicts of everyday life in a land slow to adjust to modernity, gripped by numbing tradition, poverty, and regime-enforced conformity. In the opening selection, excerpted from

Elvira Dones's novel *Stars Don't Dress Up Like That*, a young woman meditates on the circumstances of departing her homeland while evoking the sadness of her return in a haunting elegy of narrative ingenuity. Kim Mehmeti's "The Men's Council Room" employs a self-effacing narrator to lend detachment to a tale of sexual exploitation combining youthful awakening, retribution, and the supernatural. In Ylljet Aliçka's "The Slogans in Stone," a young graduate who takes a teaching post in a mountain village finds his duties include caring for a party-imposed slogan built of white-washed stones, the results of which affect not only his tenure but his life. Fatos Lubonja's "Ferit the Cow," the most outrageous character in the book, is a perennial jailbird whom incarceration cannot deter from a penchant for pilfering whatever, whenever he can, especially to sate his enormous belly. Yet running afoul of a nasty guard sends Ferit to the harshest prison, where he must atone for his shameless self-indulgence. Eqrem Basha's "The Snail's March Toward the Light of the Sun" compares a prisoner's protracted ordeal of torture to the grinding pace of a gastropod traversing his cell, deliberate, agonizing, unavailing. Finally, in Dritëro Agolli's "The Appassionata," a son's rebellion against his father's plans for his future discloses a concatenation of coincidences that tears the family apart. These stories offer a provocative glimpse into the sensibility of Europe's least-understood people, who, overcoming centuries of oppression, at long last may speak to the rest of us. — MICHAEL PINKER

BRIAN EVENSON. *THE OPEN CURTAIN*. COFFEE HOUSE PRESS, 2006. 218 PP. PAPER: $14.95.

Deep into the first section of Brian Evenson's *The Open Curtain* the reader is immersed in what seems to be little more than finely wrought genre fiction of the mystery/horror variety. Lines glow with a neon buzz of ominous and obvious foreshadowing: "You think that happens? Someone goes to see a movie about murders and then they go out and kill people?" and "People never act alone. They always drag others with them." Two narratives emerge: One involving a troubled Mormon teenager, Rudd, who is in search of his lost half-brother, Lael, his dead father's other secret son, and the second relating to Rudd's growing obsession with a 1902 murder seemingly committed by William Hooper Young, grandson of Brigham Young. Per convention, readers are told to put on their Holmesian hats to guess unfolding plots and perpetrators of impending crimes. When Rudd points out that Young's initials spell W-H-Y, one is tempted to point out that Rudd and Lael's names happen also to be an anagram for "dull read." But if the close of section one ends with a yawn at genre convention, however deftly rendered, what follows pushes beyond craft and genre into a gothic mindbender of faith, violence, and madness. The lone surviving daughter of a murdered family finds herself married to Rudd, who is prone to blackouts and attempts at self-destruction, and also happens to be her family's murderer. Evenson exploits this noir tableau to create the fraught page-turning pleasure that is the hallmark of the genre. But more significantly the author creates a psychological portrait that grows more complex and subtly rendered. Formal experimentation furthers the darkening narrative, like a repeating scene directed variously by Post-It notes, a half-brother, or a man from 1902 that may or may not have ever existed. — JOHN VINCLER

KEN KALFUS. *A DISORDER PECULIAR TO THE COUNTRY*. ECCO, 2006. 256 PP. $24.95.

Ken Kalfus' latest novel is built on a two-sided metaphor, each side carrying equal weight and casting a reciprocal shadow. On one side stands a prolonged and extremely ugly divorce. We do not learn much back-story to this divorce, how it came about or what life had been like before, but instead enter the proceedings on a day (September 11, 2001) when the couple's treatment of one another has already turned petty and cruel. We watch their cruelty grow to levels we might think absurd were it not that Kalfus, a quiet yet unflinching ironist, treats it as unexceptional, the intrinsic destructiveness of a failing domestic world. The other side of Kalfus' metaphor, then, is international current events. Starting with the terrorist attacks of 2001, the book chronicles, through the lives of its hopeless characters, the string of catastrophes that marked the early years of the 21st century: the anthrax scare, stock market collapse, Enron, the war in the Middle East. Since the divorcing couple are New Yorkers, these events both shape their lives and reflect their own crumbling humanity; it is as if the world itself has decided to join them in an orgy of willful self-destruction. Being intelligent, the characters are themselves conscious—often comically so—of the parallel courses their personal lives and world events seem to have taken, and there is a sense that, in these times, under these conditions, life could not possibly be otherwise: "But Joyce wasn't relieved. If this time the anthrax wasn't real, then why not the next? She resented her former belief that their lives in America had been secure. Someone had lied to them as shamelessly as a spouse." A palpable feeling that despair is woven into the fabric of contemporary life at all levels, that the hatred we see on television is not fundamentally separate from the hatred we experience every day, and that therefore the two sides of the divorce/catastrophe metaphor have a great deal to say to one another, is among this novel's many accomplishments. — MARTIN RIKER

RAYMOND FEDERMAN. *RETURN TO MANURE.* FC2, 2006. PAPER: $19.95.

On his blog, Raymond Federman has posted a few pictures of his recent return to the French farm where he spent World War II as a boy working for a miserable and abusive old farmer. He has posted one of himself with the rusty moldboard plow that features prominently in this story of a narrator also named Federman who spent World War II on a French farm (remember: it is always folly to assume author and narrator are the same person—in Federman's works, they have frequently been shown not to be. Thus the typical Federman statement, "I make no distinction between memory and imagination"). The angle of the photo makes discerning whether Federman is holding the plow or pissing on it difficult. And that, perhaps, is the core ambiguity of this novel. If one returns to one's past in order to deal with some old negative presence, how does one deal with it in the present? Does one merely negate the old negation and assume the result is an assertion (irony), or does one embrace that negation and in so doing turn the embrace into an assertion greater than the original negation (sincerity)? Federman plays it both ways here, and this essential ambivalence leads the narrator to an unsentimental conclusion that is as emotionally unsatisfying as it is inevitable. We, of course, see the same self-reflexivity at play here in *Return to Manure* that we do in all of Federman's major novels, but here Federman is doing something different than in his earlier novels. This is more Proust than Beckett. The narrator is seeking meaning in the flotsam of the past, and that very search, as masked as it is by Federman's tremendous humor, marks this as a significant examination into the nature and purpose of memory itself. — ECKHARD GERDES

LAIRD HUNT. *THE EXQUISITE*. COFFEE HOUSE PRESS, 2006. 256 PP. PAPER: $14.95.

To the characters that populate Laird Hunt's aptly-titled *The Exquisite*, truth is beside the point—a problematic stance for a novel that is, essentially, a murder mystery. The plot follows Henry, an unemployed and lovesick New Yorker—himself on the cusp of believability for the reader and possibly sanity—as he finds himself unwittingly joining a group of shadowy aesthetes who provide "mock-murder services" to those living in the East Village. Taking place shortly after 9/11, business is booming: people gratefully clamor for the chance to confront mortality and keep on living. At the head of the business is Aris Kindt, an eccentric old man whose namesake dates back to the dissected corpse of Rembrandt's *The Anatomy Lesson*. This personal connection to the casualties of progress frames in Kindt a kinship with those stuck on the wrong side of history and an extreme distaste for supposedly Established Truths—mock-murders are only one part of a life's devotion to what he calls "calculated falsification." Kindt challenges Henry's assumptions of normality on every topic, from the proper salt-to-oil ratio of pickled herring to the potential pleasures of lung cancer—not as a series of grotesqueries but as a radical reclaiming of aesthetics, a demand for personal, artful re-imaginings of the world. Of course, as an outsider warns Henry late in the novel, "Fake is never 100%," and it is this tension that makes *The Exquisite* such an engaging read. Each detail of Kindt's character is both revelatory and strangely suitable—

a testament to the deliberateness and precision of Hunt's sentences, yet the novel is also full of murky connections, with a plot that loosely meanders like a half-recollected dream. Ultimately, Hunt has crafted a genuine mystery novel, shifting our gaze from dénouement to the beauty of mystery itself: suffering and pleasure, without definition. — MICHAEL SQUEO

DENYS JOHNSON-DAVIES, ED. *THE ANCHOR BOOK OF MODERN ARABIC FICTION*. ANCHOR-RANDOM HOUSE, 2006. 506 PP. PAPER: $15.95.

A prolific translator who has done as much as anyone to bring modern Arabic literature to the attention of English-speaking readers, Denys Johnson-Davies has here called upon the talents of several other translators to revise and expand his earlier *Under the Naked Sky: Short Stories from the Arab World* (American University in Cairo Press, 2000). In addition to a brief but helpful Introduction and concise headnotes that will easily lead readers to further work available in translation, *The Anchor Book of Modern Arabic Fiction* collects ninety-three short stories and novel excerpts from seventy-nine writers, twenty-two of whom are women and thirty-nine of whom are, for reasons sketched in the Introduction, Egyptian. Other work comes from Algeria, Iraq, Lebanon, Libya, Morocco, Palestine, Saudi Arabia, Sudan, Syria, Tunisia, the United Arab Emirates, and Yemen. Whether reading the Libyan writer Ibrahim al-Koni's tale of a small boy whose pursuit of a malignant, magical bird ends in the boy's death or following an Iraqi woman as she plans her suicide in Daisy Al-Amir's "The Doctor's Prescription," smiling as Muhammad al Murr (United Arab Emirates) tells the story of a naïve young man whose first poem is rejected by a local newspaper or observing a woman as she begins to cope with the destruction of her Beirut home during a rocket attack in the Lebanese writer Emily Nasrallah's short story "A House Not Her Own," these stories offer great variety of style, subject matter, tone. Furthermore, they remind us that one honorable task of fiction is to offer sympathetic glimpses into the lives of others, who generally end up being more like ourselves than we might have imagined. Given the current demonizing of the Islamic world, such glimpses are more than honorable undertakings; they are also necessary ones. — BROOKE HORVATH

FRAN MASON. *HISTORICAL DICTIONARY OF POSTMODERNIST LITERATURE AND THEATER.* SCARECROW PRESS, 2007. 404 PP. $85.00.

A historical dictionary of postmodernist literature and theater is certain to generate debate on numerous levels; what is included, omitted, avoided, emphasized, and marginalized? What is offered as a point of initiation? Is a point of initiation even welcome in some respects? On many of these issues, there is much to disagree with Fran Mason's brave attempt, although I cannot imagine any structured historical dictionary that would be universally appealing. I can, however, imagine many that would be less comprehensive, inclusive, well-researched and alert to the many nuances within postmodernism. For example, Mason offers six different ways that the word postmodern is used; poststructuralist theories, a postmodern philosophical outlook, a cultural condition, a set of textual and aesthetic devices, postmodern texts that write about postmodernity in a non-experimental fashion, and the cultural products of postmodernity, more generally. This set of distinctions alone is a useful gesture to the very multiplicity of the word. Also of particular value is Mason's pointed inclusion of theater (or drama) for consideration because this wing of postmodern literature often tends to be neglected, and this may signal a point of departure for future work in this area. There are inevitably omissions that one might question, like the important critical work on one of the grand old men of postmodernist literature, Flann O'Brien, by Keith Hopper and M. Keith Booker, to name but a few. Similarly, several books on John Banville by Rüdiger Imhof, Joseph McMinn and Derek Hand are worth a mention. But this is an enormous landscape and there will always be omissions in this kind of enterprise. Mason's contribution to the field is extremely significant and should be acknowledged as such and this will be a very valuable entry point for students of postmodernist literature. — NEIL MURPHY

CHRISTINA MILLETTI. *THE RELIGIOUS & OTHER FICTIONS*. CARNEGIE MELLON UNIVERSITY PRESS, 2006. 191 PP. PAPER: $16.95.

Every so often a collection comes along that shows just how wide lean short stories can open the largest of questions. *The Religious & Other Fictions* is one such book: minimal stories, pristine in language, that don't flesh out characters and settings as a traditional story might so much as use the pleasures of the story as an act of philosophy. Reminiscent of Chekhov for their unspoken themes, for their dependence on readers to see significance between the lines, the eleven stories that make up this collection circulate around the absences that always enable belief, the multiple meanings that people have to blinder themselves to in order to be certain. "Parcel Post" alternates between Harlequin Romance-esque passages about yearning hearts and the Post-it notes that a woman leaves for a deliveryman who never delivers the "gift" she hopes for but gives her another, a fantasy that she inhabits. Here as in the other stories, both verities and lies dissolve under scrutiny. Fables reveal more truth than the fable of facts. In "Where Nööne is Now," a daughter discovers, at the moment she is to have her mother's tombstone engraved, that she never knew her real name, let alone the fate of her missing sister who may or may not have been beaten for doubting that U.S. soldiers behave more nobly than others. In the title story, memorials of memorials—that is, photos of memorials— memorialize memorializing, which is always a fiction. More to the point, in stories about a man who inherits a butcher's shop, tourists played by guides, or even the 1,000 girls living in the same apartment, Milletti's characters can never be sure if a truth, history or belief is false; or else they are oblivious to the illusionist nature of the world and only the reader is left to wonder how anyone knows what they know; how can we believe anything, especially if we have no basis for belief (unless that's what belief is)? Given the political and religious climate we live in today, these stories speak to our moment in a way that is of our moment. — STEVE TOMASULA

GOCE SMILEVSKI. *CONVERSATION WITH SPINOZA: A COBWEB NOVEL.*
TRANS. FILIP KORŽENSKI. NORTHWESTERN UNIVERSITY PRESS, 2006.
136 PP. PAPER: $16.95.

Like a cobweb, the structure of this novel is both concentric with the
narrative circling around and ending at the center and overlapping threads
that revisit key scenes and images from different directions. Framed by
the scene of Spinoza's death, throughout most of the novel the philosopher
directly addresses the entangled reader, who is encouraged to talk back. As
we might expect of a novel about a rationalist philosopher, the movement
is into the buried life of feeling and desire behind the imposing cool rigor
of Spinoza's *Ethics*, "Demonstrated in Geometrical Order." Beginning
with a straightforward account of the outward facts of Spinoza's life (with
fictional elaborations), the narrative circles back and behind to reveal the
psychological springs of his philosophy. In this case the early death of his
mother generates a sense of isolation from others that clears the space for
pure thought (philosophy). However, pure thought is symptomatic of the
very melancholy that motivates the aspiration to philosophy in the first place,
so this Spinoza circles around a small cluster of closely related biographical
incidents concerning death, sexuality and birth—in other words, philosophy
is quite simply the effort to deny mortality. As Smilevski acknowledges in his
epilogue, any such work will inevitably be tested against the understanding of
Spinoza's thought it presents. Curiously, Smilevski's Spinoza appears to be an
unreformed Descartian unable to think beyond the mind-body split, although
the adamant rejection of any such distinction is precisely the starting point of
his philosophy. Smilevski's Spinoza is familiar enough as the saintly cerebralist
aspiring to realize the "intellectual love of God," but he largely ignores the
importance of pleasure, always good for Spinoza, albeit complicated, much
less the empowerment of the body as necessary for the realization of mind,
since they are really one. Although Smilevski credits Deleuze as his primary
guide to Spinoza's thought, it is difficult to imagine how Deleuze would
recognize the Spinoza in this novel. Spinoza functions here to restage the

debate between philosophy and literature, thought and felt experience, with the former predictably coming out the loser. Whatever the shortcomings of Smilevski's reading of Spinoza—and fiction must be granted its license—this novel is a compelling dramatization of the tragedy of thought, which clearly has its fatal attraction for the author. — JEFFREY TWITCHELL-WAAS

JOSHUA FURST. *THE SABOTAGE CAFÉ*. KNOPF, 2007. 272 PP. $24.00.

Julia, the narrator of this brutal novel, has lived through the punk insanities of the 1980s. She has attempted to forget her traumatic past, to forge a "normal" suburban life; but as she tells us in her very first lines: "These things are hard to say. I'm not sure what's true and what isn't. My experience doesn't even make sense to me so I can't imagine they'll make sense to anyone else. What I can promise is that I'll be sincere." The simple, "everyday" sentences do not bode well for her or us. She is "sincere." But how can she be? She is sabotaged, traumatized by her past, and we feel uneasy about all her knowledge. Her daughter Cheryl's erratic activities upset Julia's sense of place and peace. Julia is suddenly confronted by the fact that she is suffering from Schizotypal Personality Disorder (diagnosed in 1986) and when she informs us, we don't know what to think about her motivations and observations. Thus the plain words she has given us may or may not be true. Is Cheryl really "out there" or only in Julia's mad mind? And how can we trust the story she offers? When, for example, Julia seems to see Cheryl in peril—drugs, sex, punk music—Julia simply says, "You think, when you traveled through the dark places and *survived* that the things you've learned might be transferable. They're not, though." Julia is filled with dread. And the *uncertainty principle dominates the entire novel.* As we read this "easy novel"—no complex metaphors, no nightmarish flourishes—we understand that this simple account—almost a cliché—is extremely bleak and hopeless. Julia ends the narration this way: "Searching for a way not to become me, she followed her black flag over the edge of the earth. She's never coming back." Has Julia really come back to the Sabotage Café? We are left with irresolution, no safe solution, no rest. — IRVING MALIN

DOMINIQUE FITZPATRICK-O'DINN. *TABLE OF FORMS*. SPINELESS BOOKS, 2006. 113 PP. PAPER: $12.00.

Upon seeing an exquisitely wrought statue of, say, a horse, most would see the horse, few would see the marble. So it is with sounds, crude if musical, audaciously coaxed into words. Here is a gathering of language exercises, poems that constrain language by preset obligations, intricate, inventive, demanding directives (words juxtaposed within a line must share a vowel; each line must contain all 26 letters; each successive line must contain one additional letter); here is, in short, an intemperate delight in the marble. The volume—there are no editors listed and the author's "name" is a glorious fabrication—provides a glossary should the careful eye fail to perceive the imbedded patterns. If the challenge is to uncover the design, the glossary may seem intrusive, like a tacky magician distributing a lame handbook of magic tricks to patrons during a show; but in practice the guidelines only help clarify the exotic designs (among them, liponymns, haicoups, and pangrams), like taking a backstage tour of Disneyworld. Of course, language so precisely sculpted must struggle against appearing oppressively clever—a poem that "must" use all the consonants once before repeating any can seem a sterile thing. Only newspoems collaged from current events even acknowledge the real world. What we are given, rather, is the compelling it-ness of language liberated from the tedious expectations of mimesis and narrative, language played with brio and elegance. Language thus constrained may depress some readers, like seeing some magnificent jungle animal caged. These are acts, such readers sniff, but not art. But language here is far from restrained—it is disciplined, wily, animated, resourceful, in turn nonsensical and musical, but supremely vital, dazzling to confront ("read" is not quite the verb), sculpted lines smeary with fingerprints, stunned by the audacity of their own construction. — JOSEPH DEWEY

AARON PETROVICH. *THE SESSION*. HOTEL ST. GEORGE PRESS, 2006. 64 PP. PAPER: $10.95.

"The reader sees the world through the detective's eyes," writes Paul Auster, "experiencing the proliferation of its details as if for the first time. He has become awake to the things around him, as if they might speak to him, as if, because of the attentiveness he now brings to them, they might begin to carry a meaning other than the simple fact of their existence." Auster's musings from *City of Glass*, one of the seminal literary detective stories making up his acclaimed *New York Trilogy*, aptly characterize the experience of reading Aaron Petrovich's *The Session*. This debut "novella in dialogue," hauntingly illustrated with monotypes by Vilem Benes, is the first publication from Hotel St. George Press, an imprint of Akashic Books. Unfolding like the transcript of a secretly recorded conversation, *The Session* follows the cryptic exchange of two detectives—both named Smith—who are investigating the brutal murder of the Mathematician, who has "granted definitive proof of a finite future." As the detectives spar in mock interrogation of each other, a doctor's arrival on the scene causes the reader to question everything that has happened so far. To reveal any more would give away a key source of suspense grounding this evocatively scripted detective story. Petrovich's dialogue is stark without being minimal, dramatizing the complexities of plot, character, and ontological debate with the barest of brushstrokes. It also manages to be at once grimly funny and deadly serious. Whether read as an absurdist revision of the detective genre or a novella of ideas, *The Session* joins a growing body of contemporary narratives in which investigation is a central metaphor for the struggle to master a world rife with mysteries large and small. — PEDRO PONCE

THALIA FIELD. *ULULU (CLOWN SHRAPNEL)*. COFFEE HOUSE PRESS, 2007. 256 PP. PAPER: $25.00.

When the Roundheads closed the English theaters in 1642, would-be playwrights were forced to pen closet dramas, deploying the full range of theatrical devices on paper alone. Whether motivated by some brand of contemporary Puritanism, the constraints of the capitalist market or just sheer ambitious cussedness, Thalia Field has chosen to employ the full range of 21st century media effects in creating her latest paperbound work of words. *Ululu* is structured as a three-act play, but it also draws on the conventions of opera, music, poetry, and fiction, not to mention visual arts including painting and film (treated stills by Bill Morrison, illustrations by Abbot Stranahan and an elaborate book design by Linda S. Koutsky all contribute to the total package). It seems a disservice to try to concisely describe what this remarkable book is about; suffice to say that it mainly treats the modernist myth of Lulu, a sexually unfettered character first appearing in 19th century Viennese plays and most famously portrayed by Louise Brooks in the 1929 movie *Pandora's Box*. "The law of love is better than the love of law," she's quoted as saying, which attitude is not surprisingly met with forceful repression and unpleasant consequences. The power of her persona, though, transcends the recurring tragedy that befalls her character in the many works she's inspired, so *Ululu* is Lulu's story and also the tale of the artists who've worshipped and used her, and of the cultural responses to their erotic explorations. As it unfolds (and refolds) it provides its own commentary and criticism and swallows its own tail in the process. If you wanted, you could call it a far less linear, more historically contextualized feminist version of Robert Coover's *Adventures of Lucky Pierre*, but you'd barely be scratching one of its myriad surfaces. — JAMES CROSSLEY

BRANDON STOSUY, ED. *UP IS UP, BUT SO IS DOWN: NEW YORK'S DOWNTOWN LITERARY SCENE, 1974-1992*. NEW YORK UNIVERSITY PRESS, 2006. 510 PP. PAPER: $29.95.

Part anthology, part cultural history, and replete with the requisite ephemera-cum-archival-materials needed to codify numerous social networks, fleeting events, and widely unavailable documents into an authentic historical moment, *Up Is Up, But So Is Down* is many things: a sort of dressed-down, Lower East Side version of the traditional, Manhattanite coffee table book; a punk-infused palimpsest, beautifully and carefully designed so as to look completely cobbled together; a nostalgic testament to New York City's pre-

Giuliani bohemian fin de siècle; and, most importantly, an essential and indispensable recovery-kit—a guide-by-example for how writers might give up the quest for external cultural capital and accolades from some distant and often irrelevant literary establishment, focusing instead on both honoring and enlivening one's own environs through lived and imagined experience. Stosuy's careful plundering of New York University's Downtown Collection at the Fales Library, coupled with his dedication to seeking out the actual persons involved, has paid off in the form of a virtual treasure chest full of writing that might have simply disappeared. Much of the work presented here is culled from long out-of-print journals, mimeographed magazines, self-published pamphlets, and books with little circulation outside of a small circle of initiates. The writers featured in Up Is Up, But So Is Down are the famous, infamous, forgotten, and, hopefully, those now on the cusp of long overdue recognition: Patti Smith, Richard Hell, Kathy Acker, Hal Sirowitz, Nina Zivancevic, Max Blagg, Karen Finley, Spalding Gray, Tim Dlugos, Sharon Mesmer, and David Wojnarowicz, to name but a small portion. The book itself is divided by decades, each of which includes an illuminating introduction that touches on some of the major concerns and attendant cultural shifts of the time. From the emergence of the Do-It-Yourself ethic in music and its crossover into literature in the '70s to the ravaging AIDS epidemic and the rise of French Theory in the '80s continuing into the commodification of '90s, the writing excerpted here is as often enactment as it is example of life as it was in Downtown New York City. — NOAH ELI GORDON

FRANCES WASHBURN. *ELSIE'S BUSINESS*. UNIVERSITY OF NEBRASKA PRESS, 2006. 212 PP. PAPER: $17.95.

Since Frances Washburn is professor of American Indian studies, the reader might expect her first novel, *Elsie's Business*, to deal with typical Native American themes such as the loss of culture and community. However, it proves to be not so easily classifiable. Ostensibly, the novel deals with first the rape and then years later the murder of Elsie, a half black, half Native girl who lives on the outskirts of town. What makes the novel different from both

Native American and much contemporary fiction is the way in which it plays with genre. The story comes to the reader in the form of alternating chapters, the first narrative gleaned from the fragments of Elsie's memory as she attempts to reconstruct her life after the rape, the second from an unidentified second person narrator attempting to piece together clues to Elsie's murder from the stories of an old man named Oscar DuCharme: "If you want to know more about Elsie's story than just the official reports you have to ask one of the grandfathers . . .". Just as several suspects are named in the murder, so too is the reader given several possibilities for the "you" narrator. In flirting with the mystery genre, Washburn subverts it, refusing to solve either of the mysteries (including one more dealing with the mummified remains of a child). In so doing, Washburn writes the truest Native American novel. Though she rejects the typical Native subject matter, the structure of her story embraces the deepest Native traditions in their oblique approach to "truth." Just as so many of Oscar's stories seem to be digressions, as in the story of *Inktomi* the spider: "a story that you think has nothing to do with Elsie," or the story of the starving people: "'It isn't about *that*,' he says. 'It's a story about how the crows became black,'" the reader soon realizes that there are no answers to questions such as murder and identity. For a culture that has lost nearly everything, what does it matter who is to blame? What matters is that the story is passed on. It is enough that the narrator hears Elsie's business, that we hear her story. Leave it to others to uncover mere facts. — PETER GRANDBOIS

DELILLO FIEDLER GASS PYNCHON
University of Delaware Press
Collections on Contemporary Masters

UNDERWORDS
Perspectives on Don DeLillo's *Underworld*

Edited by Joseph Dewey, Steven G. Kellman, and Irving Malin

Essays by Jackson R. Bryer, David Cowart, Kathleen Fitzpatrick, Joanne Gass, Paul Gleason, Donald J. Greiner, Robert McMinn, Thomas Myers, Ira Nadel, Carl Ostrowski, Timothy L. Parrish, Marc Singer, and David Yetter

$39.50

INTO *THE TUNNEL*
Readings of Gass's Novel

Edited by Steven G. Kellman and Irving Malin

Essays by Rebecca Goldstein, Donald J. Greiner, Brooke Horvath, Marcus Klein, Jerome Klinkowitz, Paul Maliszewski, James McCourt, Arthur Saltzman, Susan Stewart, and Heide Ziegler

$35.00

LESLIE FIEDLER AND AMERICAN CULTURE

Edited by Steven G. Kellman and Irving Malin

Essays by John Barth, Robert Boyers, James M. Cox, Joseph Dewey, R.H.W. Dillard, Geoffrey Green, Irving Feldman, Leslie Fiedler, Susan Gubar, Jay L. Halio, Brooke Horvath, David Ketterer, R.W.B. Lewis, Sanford Pinsker, Harold Schechter, Daniel Schwarz, David R. Slavitt, Daniel Walden, and Mark Royden Winchell

$36.50

PYNCHON AND *MASON & DIXON*

Edited by Brooke Horvath and Irving Malin

Essays by Jeff Baker, Joseph Dewey, Bernard Duyfhuizen, David Foreman, Donald J. Greiner, Brian McHale, Clifford S. Mead, Arthur Saltzman, Thomas H. Schaub, David Seed, and Victor Strandberg

$39.50

ORDER FROM ASSOCIATED UNIVERSITY PRESSES
2010 Eastpark Blvd., Cranbury, New Jersey 08512
PH 609-655-4770   FAX 609-655-8366   E-mail AUP440@ aol.com

NINTH
LETTER

www.ninthletter.com

RECENTLY FEATURING
NEW WRITINGS BY

Oscar Hijuelos

William Wenthe

Lucia Perillo

L.S. Asekoff

Michael Martone

Sheryl St. Germain

Cate Marvin

Ruth Ellen Kocher

Geri Doran

Robin Hemley

Steve Stern

PUBLISHED **SEMI-ANNUALLY** IN **MAY** AND **DECEMBER**

NINTH LETTER › DEPARTMENT OF ENGLISH › UNIVERSITY OF ILLINOIS
608 S. WRIGHT ST. › URBANA, IL 61801

Dalkey Archive
Scholarly Series

Don't Ever Get Famous:
Essays on New York Writing
after the New York School
DANIEL KANE

Reading Games:
An Aesthetics of Play in
Flann O'Brien, Samuel Beckett, and Georges Perec
KIMBERLY BOHMAN-KALAJA

Rayner Heppenstall:
A Critical Study
G. J. BUCKELL

Fever Vision:
The Life and Works of
Coleman Dowell
EUGENE HAYWORTH

The Paradox of Freedom:
A Study of the Life and Writings
of Nicholas Mosley
SHIVA RAHBARAN

Energy of Delusion:
A Book on Plot
VIKTOR SHKLOVSKY

The Walk:
Notes on a Romantic Image
JEFFREY C. ROBINSON

I am Otherwise:
The Romance between Poetry and
Theory after the Death of the Subject
ALEX E. BLAZER

The essays in this book focus attention on the vibrant New York poetry scene of the 1960s and '70s, on the poets who came after what is now known as the New York School. Amiri Baraka, Bernadette Mayer, Hannah Weiner, Clark Coolidge, Anne Waldman, and Ron Padgett are just some of the poets who extended the line that John Ashberry, Frank O'Hara, Kenneth Koch, and James Schuyler started. In *Don't Ever Get Famous*, a range of writers and scholars examine the cultural, sociological, and historical contexts of this wildly diverse group of writers. These poets, many of whom are still writing today, changed American poetry forever, and this book provides the first large-scale consideration of their work.

Don't Ever Get Famous:
Essays on New York Writing
after the New York School

DANIEL KANE

Dalkey Archive Scholarly Series
Literary Criticism
$34.95 / paper
ISBN-13: 978-1-56478-460-5

"Kane's volume is the first to tackle the period in New York's downtown literary history most closely tied to the group of poets known as the 'Second Generation New York School.' . . . [It] is a must-have for historians of American poetry in the 20th century."
—*Publishers Weekly*

"It was the historian Johan Huizinga who first elaborated a theory of play. Martin Heidegger, Ludwig Wittgenstein, Roger Caillot and other luminaries have also been drawn to the subject. Now, Kimberly Bohman-Kalaja has applied play-theory to the works of three authors - Flann O'Brien, Samuel Beckett and Georges Perec, with illuminating, sometimes startling results. I was in turn bemused, enlightened and exhilarated by the realization of what adept game-players these authors were."

—Anthony Cronin, author of *Samuel Beckett: The Last Modernist* and *No Laughing Matter: The Life and Times of Flann O'Brien*

Reading Games:
An Aesthetics of Play in Flann O'Brien, Samuel Beckett, and Georges Perec

KIMBERLY BOHMAN-KALAJA

Dalkey Archive Scholarly Series
Literary Criticism
$34.95 / paper
ISBN-13: 978-1-56478-473-5

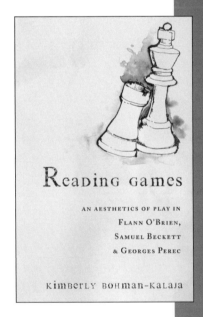

"We all know that there's more to games than fun. Bohman-Kalaja's remarkable study of O'Brien, Beckett and Perec is the first to get to grips with the deeper issues involved in the ludic practices of these post-modern masters. It also teaches us a great deal about what kind of games can be played with and through words. Learned, illuminating, original and profound, this is a study that should transform the teaching of modern literature—and bring back some of the fun!"

—David Bellos

This book examines the first five novels of Rayner Heppenstall (1911-1981). During his lifetime, many critics cited Heppenstall as the founder of the nouveau roman, believing his debut novel, *The Blaze of Noon* (1939), anticipated the post-war innovations of French writers such as Alain Robbe-Grillet and Nathalie Sarraute. Since his death, however, Heppenstall's reputation has faded, and his fiction is out of print. His final novels, written during a descent into madness, were structurally simplistic and politically unpalatable, and their disastrous critical reception clouded critical judgment of his previous novels. G.J. Buckell examines the importance of technical experimentation, rather than the ideological content, within Heppenstall's earlier works, and seeks a more favorable standing for Heppenstall within our critical and cultural memory.

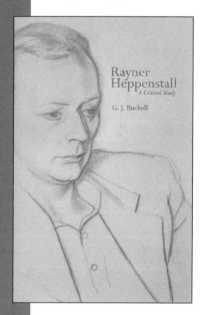

Rayner Heppenstall:
A Critical Study

G. J. BUCKELL

Dalkey Archive Scholarly Series
Literary Criticism
$29.95 / paper
ISBN: 978-1-56478-471-1

"Heppenstall's novels were poetic, considered, and intelligently realised engagements with literary form, and, regardless of the sub-discourses of Modernist writing they can justifiably be situated within, they deserve a far better reputation."

—*G. J. Buckell*

From his birth in rural Kentucky during the Great Depression to his suicide in Manhattan in 1985, Coleman Dowell played many roles. He was a songwriter and lyricist for television. He was a model. He was a Broadway playwright. He served in the U.S. Army, both abroad and at home. And most notably, he was the author of novels that Edmund White, among others, has called "masterpieces." But Dowell was deeply troubled by a deperssion that hung over him his entire life. Pegged as both a Southern writer and a gay writer, he loathed such categorization, preferring to be judged only by his work. *Fever Vision* describes one of the most tormented, talented, and inventive writers of recent American literature, and shows how his eventful life contributed to the making of his incredible art.

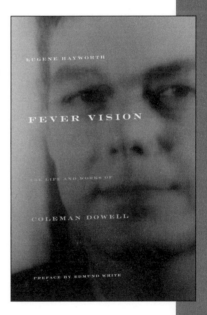

Fever Vision:
The Life and Works of Coleman Dowell

Eugene Hayworth

Dalkey Archive Scholarly Series
A Biography
$24.95 / paper
ISBN: 978-1-56478-457-5

"Gene Hayworth has done his homework by interviewing surviving family members and friends and by reading early drafts and letters and everything unpublished that the estate has made available. . . . This is a cautionary tale, perhaps—though what it mainly seems to be cautioning us against is a sentiment that overtakes most people with time: disappointment."
—*Edmund White,*
from the Introduction

RECEIVE 25% OFF ON ORDERS
PLACED BEFORE OCTOBER 30, 2007

As the first book-length study of Nicholas Mosley, *The Paradox of Freedom* combines a discussion of the author's incredible biography with an investigation of his writing. The son of Oswald Mosley, a British Lord, a Christian convert, a war veteran, a voracious reader, and an important thinker, Nicholas Mosley has employed all of these experiences and ideas in novels and memoirs that seek to describe the paradoxical nature of freedom: how can man be free when limiting structures are necessary? The answer lies in the ways telling and retelling stories allow one to escape the seemingly logical boundaries of life and discover new meanings and possibilities. This is a much-needed companion to the work of one of Britain's most important post-War writers.

The Paradox of Freedom:
A Study of the Life and Writings of Nicholas Mosley

Shiva Rahbaran

Dalkey Archive Scholarly Series
Literary Criticism
$29.95 / paper
ISBN: 978-1-56478-488-9

"Nicholas Mosley is one of the most intellectually stimulating, imaginative and occasionally perplexing of contemporary novelists. We have long needed a critical study of his work in all its range and variety, and Shiva Rahbaran has now supplied this. Her study of Mosley's fiction is distinguished by the intelligence of her appreciation and the sympathy of her approach. It will be of great value to students and the common reader alike."

—Allan Massie

One of the greatest literary minds of the twentieth century, Viktor Shklovsky writes the critical equivalent of what Ross Chambers calls "loiterature"—writing that roams, playfully digresses, moving freely between the literary work and the world. In *Energy of Delusion*, a masterpiece that Shklovsky worked on over thirty years, he turns his unique critical sensibility to Tolstoy's life and novels, applying the famous "formalist method" he invented in the 1920s to Tolstoy's massive body of work, and at the same time taking Tolstoy (as well as Boccaccio, Pushkin, Chekhov, Dostoevsky, and Tugenev) as a springboard to consider the devices of literature—how novels work and what they do.

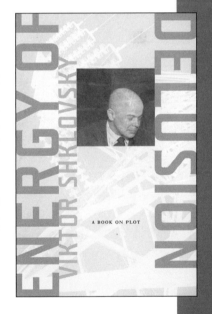

Energy of Delusion:
A Book on Plot

Viktor Shklovsky
Translation by
Shushan Avagyan

Dalkey Archive Scholarly Series
Literary Criticism
$14.95 / paper
ISBN: 978-1-56478-426-1

"A rambling, digressive stylist, Shklovsky throws off brilliant aperçus on every page ... Like an architect's blueprint, [he] lays bare the joists and studs that hold up the house of fiction."
—*Michael Dirda, Washington Post*

"Perhaps because he is such an unlikely Tolstoyan, Viktor Shklovsky's writing on Tolstoy is always absorbing and often brilliant."
—*Russian Review*

The Walk, a meditation on walking and on the literature of walking, ruminates on this pervasive, even commonplace, modern image. It is not so much an argument as a journey along the path of literature, noting the occasions and settings, the pleasures and possibilities of different types of walking, and the many literatures walking has produced. Jeffrey C. Robinson's discussion is less criticism than appreciation. With an autobiographical bent, he leads the reader through Romantic, modern, and contemporary literature to show us the shared pleasures of reading, writing, and walking.

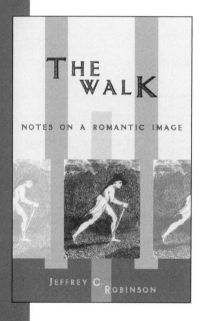

The Walk:
Notes on a Romantic Image

JEFFREY C. ROBINSON
AFTERWORD BY ROGER GILBERT

Dalkey Archive Scholarly Series
Literary Criticism
$19.95 / paper
ISBN: 978-1-56478-459-9

"Jeffrey C. Robinson's *The Walk* is a lively and intelligent omnibus for thinkers as well as for walkers. His evident love of literature is a genuine enthusiasm for all that is best in life."
—Annie Dillard

"The Walk is a stunning, revealing, and thought-provoking revision of Romantic studies, one that forces us to reexamine the conditions of our own lives and minds."
—*Wordsworth Circle*

I Am Otherwise: The Romance between Poetry and Theory after the Death of the Subject examines the contemporary poet's relationship with language in the age of theory. As the book works through close readings and interpretations of Adrienne Rich and Harold Bloom, John Ashbery and Paul de Man, Jorie Graham and Maurice Blanchot, and Barrett Watten and Jacques Lacan, it shows how the main psychological modes of contemporary poetry and the postmodern poet are anxiety, irony, abjection, and destitution. The book ultimately concludes that the new theoretical poetry self-consciously renders the effect of critical theory in its own construction. Whereas poets of the past tarried with nature, self, or philosophy, poets of our time unite lyric feeling with literary theory itself.

I Am Otherwise:
The Romance between Poetry and Theory after the Death of the Subject

ALEX E. BLAZER

Dalkey Archive Scholarly Series
Literary Criticism
$34.95 / paper
ISBN: 978-1-56478-458-2

I AM OTHERWISE:
THE ROMANCE BETWEEN
POETRY AND THEORY
AFTER THE DEATH
OF THE SUBJECT

ALEX E. BLAZER

"Like Ashbery, I too am nostalgic for an understanding of subjectivity—replete with inner being, in control of the outer language—which current thinking does not afford."
—Alex E. Blazer

ORDER FORM

Individuals may use this form to subscribe to the *Review of Contemporary Fiction* or to order back issues of the *Review* and Dalkey Archive titles at a discount (see below for details).

Title	ISBN	Quantity	Price

Subtotal _____

Less Discount _____
(10% for one book, 20% for two or more books and
25% for Scholarly titles advertised in this issue)

Subtotal _____

Plus Postage _____
(domestic: $3 + $1 per book / foreign: $5 + $3 per book)

1 Year Individual Subscription to the **Review** _____
($17 domestic, $20.50 foreign)

Total _____

Mailing Address _____

_____

_____

_____

xxvi/3

Credit card payment ☐ Visa ☐ Mastercard

Acct. # _____ Exp. Date _____

Name on card _____ Phone # _____

Please make checks (in U.S. dollars only) payable to *Dalkey Archive Press*

mail or fax this form to: Dalkey Archive Press, University of Illinois,
605 E. Springfield Avenue, MC–475, Champaign, IL 61820
fax: 217.244.9142; *tel:* 217.244.5700